CW01636545

JUST O

(A PORCH BY THE SEA—BOOK 1)

SOPHIE LOVE

Sophie Love

#1 bestselling author Sophie Love is author of THE INN AT SUNSET HARBOR romantic comedy series, which includes eight books; of THE ROMANCE CHRONICLES romantic comedy series, which includes 5 books; of the CANINE CASPER cozy mystery series, which includes six books (and counting); of the CURIOUS BOOKSTORE cozy mystery series, which includes five books (and counting); and of the new A PORCH BY THE SEA romantic comedy series, which includes five books (and counting).

Sophie would love to hear from you, so please visit www.sophieloveauthor.com to email her, to join the mailing list, to receive free ebooks, to hear the latest news, and to stay in touch!

ISBN: 978-1-0943-8125-1

BOOKS BY SOPHIE LOVE

A PORCH BY THE SEA
JUST ONE KISS (Book #1)
JUST ONE CHANCE (Book #2)
JUST ONE SUMMER (Book #3)
JUST ONE NIGHT (Book #4)
JUST ONE DAY (Book #5)

A CURIOUS BOOKSTORE COZY MYSTERY
THE WITCHING PLACE: A FATAL FOLIO (Book #1)
THE WITCHING PLACE: MURDER BY MANUSCRIPT (Book #2)
THE WITCHING PLACE: A PERILOUS PAGE (Book #3)
THE WITCHING PLACE: A VANISHED VOLUME (Book #4)
THE WITCHING PLACE: A TAINTED TOME (Book #5)

THE CANINE CASPER COZY MYSTERY SERIES
THE GHOSTLY GROUNDS: MURDER AND BREAKFAST (Book #1)
THE GHOSTLY GROUNDS: DEATH AND BRUNCH (Book #2)
THE GHOSTLY GROUNDS: MALICE AND LUNCH (Book #3)
THE GHOSTLY GROUNDS: VENGEANCE AND DINNER (Book #4)
THE GHOSTLY GROUNDS: SCANDAL AND SUPPER (Book #5)
THE GHOSTLY GROUNDS: DISASTER AND DESSERT (Book #6)

THE INN AT SUNSET HARBOR
FOR NOW AND FOREVER (Book #1)
FOREVER AND FOR ALWAYS (Book #2)
FOREVER, WITH YOU (Book #3)
IF ONLY FOREVER (Book #4)
FOREVER AND A DAY (Book #5)
FOREVER, PLUS ONE (Book #6)
FOR YOU, FOREVER (Book #7)
CHRISTMAS FOREVER (Book #8)

THE ROMANCE CHRONICLES
LOVE LIKE THIS (Book #1)
LOVE LIKE THAT (Book #2)

LOVE LIKE OURS (Book #3)
LOVE LIKE THEIRS (Book #4)
LOVE LIKE YOURS (Book #5)

CHAPTER ONE

"Get out."

Two words Emma Adams never thought she'd say to the love of her life. But now, as she stared at him—his unapologetic face, his eyes cold and haughty—she knew they were the right words. She felt the power of them lift the barest bit of the lancing pain that had invaded her heart.

Troy crossed his arms over his gym-sculpted chest and rolled his eyes at her. "You're being dramatic. I don't know where you're getting this from."

Her husband looked so right in their formal living room, perfectly the part in his designer workout gear, not a hair out of place in his impeccably undercut hair. Emma took a mental inventory of the room to try to calm her anger. High-end furniture. Emma's own paintings on the neutral walls, tastefully lit. Big-screen TV built in to the expansive bookcases that took up the far wall. The small bar with retro signs that held Troy's whiskey collection and Emma's preferred vintages of wine. It looked like a picture out of *House Lovely* magazine. It looked like the kind of place where people like Emma and Troy should be *happy*.

Except, Troy wasn't. He'd found happiness in another place, with another *woman*. The mystery woman who could provide him with so much more than Emma could.

Emma breezed past him and snatched her purse up from where she'd dropped it when she'd come in from work. She fished out her phone and tossed the purse onto their cream-colored suede sectional. A few swipes later, and she turned the phone toward her husband.

Keeping her voice even, somehow, she said, "Two thousand dollars at Lush Jewelry last month?"

The credit card statement glowed from the phone screen, a cold, unchangeable fact.

Emma continued. "It's not my birthday, nor your mother's, and it's nowhere near Christmas."

Troy's snort was emphatic—and his eyes darted anywhere but Emma's own. "Please. A man can't surprise his wife with a gift?"

Emma felt her lips curve in a triumphant smile. How was it she'd known he would try that lame excuse? She clicked to the next page of the statement and zoomed in on the four-hundred-dollar restaurant charge.

"Of course. He can also take her to *Chez Fantaisie*, which has a waiting list of three months to get a table during dinner hours. How nice of you to reserve that for us. Funny that you didn't mention it when you went last week, the very evening of the day I left for the conference. Was that part of the surprise you had for me?"

Troy's face paled under his tan.

"Should I keep going?" she asked, waving her phone. "Lingerie, spa services, handbags…"

"You're crazy. You're *snooping on me*?" Troy threw up his hands and turned, stomping toward their bedroom. She didn't give chase.

"It's a joint account, Troy," Emma explained, staying put in the family room. "Maybe next time, check which card you're handing over *before* you wine and dine your other woman."

His voice, somewhat muffled with the distance between them, came back, incensed. "I don't have to put up with this." There was the sound of a zipper, and then the opening and closing of drawers.

"Exactly my sentiments," Emma said mock-cheerfully, kicking off her high heels. She usually never wore her heels past the front door—Troy always griped that the thin stilettos might ruin the expensive carpeting that padded the first floor.

But now, as she kicked the shoes off, she was heedless of anything from her day that may have remained on the shoes—anything that might smudge the pristine flooring. The absence of their height dropped Emma from her work-assertive five-six to a more diminutive five-three. But she already felt small due to her unwelcome discoveries about Troy's activities over the past week, and so she didn't really clock the step-down that usually amused her.

Troy reappeared in the living room, big, rolling suitcase in hand. "You know, Emma, maybe you wouldn't be so paranoid if you weren't always gone for work. If we had a better emotional connection."

She lifted her chin. "Paranoia doesn't charge twenty dollars for an after-dinner martini. But *Chez Fantaisie* does. Remind me—when did you start drinking candy apple martinis, Troy?"

He yanked the handle of the rolling bag and pushed open the door to the garage, which was just off the family room. Emma heard the garage door hum open. Troy's tone was dripping with condescension when he replied.

"Listen, if you want to stay with me, you should consider going to counseling."

"Me? You mean couple's counseling?"

"No, just you," he retorted.

Emma couldn't help the short, barking laugh that escaped her. Troy's mouth dropped open, and he stared at her, aghast. Suffice it to say that laughing at him had not been her usual response when he'd pulled the huffy exit-the-house move on prior occasions.

"Do you not understand, Emma? I'm *leaving*," he pressed, pausing in the doorway.

Emma propped her bare feet on the coffee table. "Please," she said coldly, "leave. Or maybe I should say, *be her guest*."

She waved an airy hand in his direction.

"I-I'll be at my parents' house," he replied weakly. Then, after another long moment during which she assumed he was waiting to see if she would beg him to stay, Troy left, slamming the door to the garage behind him.

"*Au revoir*," she hollered at the closed garage door.

Emma managed to keep herself composed and waited until she heard his sports car roar out of the driveway before she let the tears come.

***

Softees tissues—absorbent enough to soak up all your post-cheating tears!

Emma blew her nose into "the world's softest tissue" for about the hundredth time in the past two hours. One of the perks of her job at VogueThink Marketing was that clients often delivered an abundance of products to the office. She'd never imagined she would need twelve *cases*—but now she had a use for the ones that'd been sitting in her garage since last Christmas.

She'd been a sobbing, snotty mess since Troy had stormed out, but once the plush luxuriousness of Softees had hit her cheeks, she'd at least become a dry, sobbing mess.

If only tissues could solve the problem of her husband's empty dresser drawers.

"He didn't even seem *sorry* about it," Emma blubbered into the phone, trying to catch her breath.

There was momentary silence on the other end of the line, and then Emma heard her sister take a deep breath. "Babe, I'm trying really hard not to say, 'I told you so,' but Troy has been a player—and kind of a jerk—since high school. You have always been so much better than he is as a person. I can't believe it's taken him this long to show his true colors."

Emma dissolved into a fresh flood of tears. "All those years down the drain! I *hate* him." She rose from the cream-colored sectional and drifted toward the kitchen. "I'm going to become a hermit now. Hide in the house. Work from home indefinitely. Pajamas all day. No video conferencing. I'm getting a cat—no, *several.*"

"Don't get a cat just yet. Don't you have a reunion tomorrow?" Morgan asked as Emma's bare feet touched the cool marble tile in the kitchen.

Emma yanked the towering, stainless steel fridge door open to rummage through takeout containers and way too many condiment bottles. She snuffled deeply, her voice thick because of her now-stuffy nose. "Tell me why I'm going to go to my fifteen-year reunion the day after I find out my husband's cheating on me."

"Because you're Emma Adams. Advertising queen of Los Angeles. I mean, speaking of cats, I still see the *cat food* ad you came up with pop up on my social media. Some competing law firm here even spoofed it on a billboard. You are the mover for all the big-name shakers."

You Gotta be Kitten Me. It had been pretty good work, had gone viral within a day, and launched her advertising career—even if it had put a few other dreams on hold.

Emma chewed on her thumbnail. "What if someone asks where he is?"

"Tell them he's probably with his mistress. He was a big king, untouchable sports honcho when he was a teenager, Emma. The real world doesn't work like the hallways of Haven High. You can do some serious damage to his reputation. I hear that Cindy Brown from Haven actually quit lawyering and has a pretty successful gossip vlog now. Maybe she'd out Troy for the weasel he is. Didn't he once trip her in the lunchroom on purpose?"

Emma winced, recalling the day clearly. Junior year. A dare from one of his football teammates. She located a Chinese takeout container that passed the smell test, closed the fridge door, and went to sit at one of the barstools at the massive kitchen island. "Yes. I remember checking on her after—and he never apologized then either."

Her sister's next sigh came heavily over the line. "You want to come stay with us for a bit?"

After a bite of noodles and some consideration, Emma said, "No, no..."

"Emma."

"Morgan."

Emma caught her own reflection in the doors of the fridge as the conversation came to a standstill. There were circles under her wide, blue eyes as a result of the past hours of crying. Her French twist was partly undone, wisps of blonde hair tangled at her temples and her nape. She was still in her skirt suit from work, and she suddenly felt the constriction of her waistband and her suit jacket.

It was the same feeling she'd had, in varying degrees, over her years with Troy. A slow simmer of anger began to replace her sadness. Plonking her phone on the island, she switched it to speaker and pulled at the buttons of her jacket.

"Fine. I'll get a good night's sleep, and I'll go to the reunion."

Morgan squealed on the other end. "Atta girl. You know, Eddie Stanhope might be there."

Emma's face flushed as she tossed her jacket onto the dining room table, thinking of the cute, sandy-haired guy who she'd crushed on for years before Troy had come into her life. "Yeah, maybe. I know Trish is going, so even if everything else is a bust, I can cry on her shoulder."

"Good attitude. That's what best friends are for. Now, I hate to bail, but we have to be up early for soccer."

"Go. Mom-ing comes before my crumbling life," Emma quipped.

"Hush. You know I'm here for you always. In fact, when you're ready, if you want to talk about your next steps, I'm here."

Emma felt a small but genuine smile touch her lips, even though the thought *of next steps*—which she knew was a lawyer and the dissolution of her life and home—scared her. "Thank you. I love you."

"Love you too."

When the screen showed the call ended, Emma's smile wavered, then fell, and she dropped her forehead to the cool top of the island, tears welling.

She let herself stay that way for the count of ten, and then she sat up, snatched up her phone, and went to take a shower. On the way, she snagged a bottle of wine and a glass from the rack she'd stared at during the earlier fight.

After two glasses of wine in very short order, Emma stepped into a too-hot shower, where she scrubbed herself pink to try to erase the crawling feeling that covered her from head to toe. She dressed in her comfiest pajamas, slipped on a pair of hiking boots that she found in the back of her closet, and went straight to the cabinet that held Troy's collection of expensive alcohol.

She used a basket from the laundry room to gather up every bottle, and then took the basket to the backyard, where the dusk was just settling over the city, sending sparkles of waning light over the surface of their expansive inground swimming pool. The pool was artfully done in mosaic tiles and had a waterfall feature. One side of the pool was covered in water jets that could be turned on to cast a spray of water that arced impressively over half the pool. The whole effect was one of affluence and luxury, and Emma hated it.

After she'd dragged one of the trash bins from the back deck, she picked up one of the whiskey bottles—and remembering vividly how Troy had gloated that this single bottle had cost several hundred dollars—Emma uncapped the top, walked numbly to the edge of the pool, and turned over the heavily chlorinated water. The booze and pool chemicals combined to make her eyes water. Then, she dropped the empty bottle into the trash, and glass exploded over the bottom of the bin, the sound musical but chaotic.

How dare he, she thought as she emptied the second bottle. The same week he'd bought the red label bottle in her hand had been the week he'd forgotten her birthday.

More broken glass in the bin, and then more with the third bottle, and then the fourth—she threw them each into the trash can with increasing force, sobbing louder with each smash, not caring that the next-door neighbor's back floodlights had come on and the smell of spilled whiskey was strong enough to sting her already burning eyes.

Emma hadn't even *wanted* this house. It was too big for just the two of them, and she'd wanted a backyard instead of the sun deck and pool, which sat unused ninety-nine percent of the time. But Troy loved the location, the zip code, the proximity to the rich and famous.

She made it through a dozen whiskey bottles, staring when she was done at the trash bin full of broken shards. The can was smooth and unblemished on the outside but full of shattered bits under the lid. Well, if *that* didn't perfectly symbolize her broken marriage, she didn't know what did. Then, spinning on her booted heel, sprinkles of errant broken glass crunching under her sole, she carried the empty laundry basket back toward the sliding glass doors. Next were Troy's watches—and then, maybe she'd start on the fancy workout equipment that filled the garage.

Emma made sure to turn her phone off when she passed it on the kitchen island. If things followed the same pattern as their previous fights, Troy would be calling her in the next hour, apologizing while slipping in subtle hints that she was crazy—no way had he been flirting, and that phone number in his gym bag was just a potential training client. She had fallen for it so many times.

But she wouldn't answer.

Not tonight. And not tomorrow, when she would enjoy the reunion where he hopefully wouldn't show his face.

It would be Troy's turn to wonder where *she* was.

Anger rose and rose inside Emma, unabated by the destruction of the whiskey bottles. Next up were Troy's designer watches, for all the time he had stolen from her.

And then, she would see what she had to wear for the reunion.

CHAPTER TWO

The venue where Haven High's fifteenth reunion was being held was splashy, in true Los Angeles style. Why they had chosen to host the reunion outside of Haven by the Sea, Emma would never know, but it stood to reason that many of her past peers had migrated outside of the small town. And Emma was grateful not to have to make the flight or drive back, considering the circumstances.

Emma's heart beat hard as the doorman opened the heavy, shiny golden doors that fronted the Stargazer Resort in downtown LA. She'd been nervous enough to skip driving herself, instead opting for a rideshare to the swanky hotel.

Her first glimpse inside the Stargazer took her breath away. The building had been, at one point in the 1940s, a shoe factory. It had gone through various incarnations over the years, until the hotel had taken ownership about twenty years back. Inside, a welcoming foyer with a ceiling that went all the way up to the industrial steel beams of the roof gave the impression of a chic, city loft—and crystal chandeliers dripped from those beams, heavy with cut gems that threw tiny rainbows on the rough brick walls. A check-in clerk in a retro uniform, the dark-red jacket studded with shining gold buttons, smiled a greeting from the deep mahogany reception desk.

Emma shook off her nervousness, tugged at the hem of her new, slinky, red dress, and smiled back at him.

"Haven High reunion?" she asked.

"Right away, ma'am," the man said.

Instead of just pointing her to the proper hallway, he rang a small bell, and a younger man dressed in the same fancy uniform appeared. Emma found herself with an offered elbow, a dazzling smile—the second man could easily star in any toothpaste ad she'd seen over her years in marketing—and an escort to the exact place she needed to be.

Once her helper had ushered her into the Monarch Ballroom, he disappeared with the same quickness he'd appeared, leaving only a lingering trail of some very nice cologne. Emma was left standing, clutching her small evening bag, right in front of the check-in table for the reunion.

She wasn't sure if she was thankful for her quick arrival, or if dawdling a little would have calmed her anxiety.

Oh, well. You're here, now.

Emma looked around the crowded ballroom, where a center-placed dance floor was circled with tall cocktail tables swathed in linens. She didn't see her best friend, Trish. Maybe Trish would come in late—that was certainly her style.

Squaring her shoulders, Emma looked over at the woman at the check-in table. She marched that way, as wide a smile plastered on her face as she could manage, and chirped, "Emma Adams."

Then, as the woman searched for—and quickly located—her name tag, Emma asked, "Do you think you could do me a favor on that last name…?"

***

"Ohmygash, but seriously. *Where* is Tray?" The woman with the teased red hair smacked her gum again and swirled a cocktail sword through her piña colada.

"Troy," Emma gritted out. As she had predicted, all anyone had asked her about since she'd arrived at the reunion was her husband—and now, for about the twentieth time, she was floundering for an excuse.

The one she'd used most often was *He couldn't get out of work*—which was so far from the truth. Troy hadn't worked since his trust fund had kicked in at twenty-one, preferring to "network" with his father's Hollywood contacts, which meant long lunches with celebrities at trendy restaurants and parties at producer's houses. What luck, to have a father who owned the biggest vineyard in Haven by the Sea, California.

Propping her chin in her hand, Emma looked around the ballroom. It was decorated to mimic the theme of their senior prom, which had been "Under the Sea." Teal, gold, and sandy bronze were the colors of the evening, and the hotel had definitely upgraded from the balloon arches of her youth to swanky, draping fabric and arrangements of real seashells and glittering tulle. The low lights drew attention to the candles on each table, which flickered out of candleholders layered with sand and beach glass. It was pretty, to be sure—but Emma didn't really want the flashback to her younger days.

She wished that Trish would come, already. Her childhood bestie still hadn't shown her perfectly made up face yet, and Emma desperately wanted someone to gossip and sleuth with over the identity of Troy's mystery mistress.

Maybe this hadn't been such a good idea, coming to the reunion. Maybe she should just leave and hire a PI to sift through the credit card statements and phone records and pinpoint who Troy's trollop was. Maybe Trish was becoming one more person in Emma's life who would treat her like an afterthought.

Great.

She and Trish hadn't seen each other much over the past fifteen years, with Emma's work and travel and Trish's busy catering company, though they had managed dinners or coffees when Trish's work allowed her the odd free weekday.

Realistically, Emma knew she could turn her phone on and text Trish to find out her ETA, but she wouldn't—because she was afraid of the messages she might have from Troy. And her in-laws, *ugh*. Emma shuddered at the memory of the speech that her mother-in-law gave every time Emma and Troy came to the precipice of breaking up—phrases like *keeping up appearances*, and *men will be men* made acid rise in Emma's throat.

And his text messages would be like a broken record, too. Messages just like he'd sent after every one of their past fights. Messages that had caused her to cave with their promises of "doing better" and "changing."

This time, she didn't believe him.

The star quarterback.

The one who all the girls had wanted.

The man she'd loved for the last decade and a half, blind to the faults that were now so glaring. And yet, her heart still pinched at the thought of what her life might be like without him.

Double ugh.

The woman standing at the conference room bar smiled a wobbly smile and swirled the cocktail sword again. "Oh, yeah. Troy. He was a looker. And you snagged him soooo early. Lucky!" The woman drew out the "y" on the end of the word in a way that was like a cheese grater on Emma's last remaining nerve.

"Yeah. That's me. Lucky. If you'll excuse me..." Emma grabbed her own drink—which was the same glass of wine she'd been nursing for the past hour—and slid away from the bar. Her head throbbed.

Emma set her wine glass on a nearby accent table and looked for the nearest exit to step outside for some air. She needed to clear her head.

She couldn't go through the middle of the dance floor, which was surrounded by the accent tables at the back of the room, forming a cozy semicircle. No way did she want to get dragged in to the Electric Slide or have to Tootsie Roll with her old Home Ec. teacher. Deciding the edges of the crowded dance floor were safest, she weaved around the people throwing their hands in the air like they just didn't care, persisting until she got to the ballroom door.

Emma had just stepped out of the ballroom and into the hallway when a familiar voice rang out.

"Emma! Girl, over here!"

Relief flooded her. Trish was jogging lightly down the plushly carpeted hall. She was dragging the same magazine-model bellhop who had escorted Emma an hour prior, and the poor guy looked half-lovestruck and half-afraid. The mood lighting in the hallway glowed over the top of Trish's dark-brown hair, worn loose, and curling over her shoulders like Emma's own. Trish was dressed to party in a form-fitting black dress and a pair of heels that had sparkly ankle straps. Her wide, beaming smile stretched impossibly wider as Emma hurried to meet her.

There was so much to tell Trish. She was the perfect person for Emma to vent her frustrations. She'd known both Emma and Troy since childhood, and Trish had been a constant in Emma's young life. Seeing her now, at this point of personal crisis, made Emma ache for the time they had lost over their adult years.

Troy would be out of Emma's life soon. It was time for her to solidly reconnect with the people she had lost a true connection with in her years with him.

Emma met Trish just past the ballroom doors, running into her friend's tight hug. It felt good. It felt like everything was going to be all right. When Emma pulled back, she realized that Trish was still holding onto the bellhop, who had been awkwardly half-pulled into their embrace. Trish untangled her arm from his and patted his cheek.

"Thank you so much, Jack. You're a doll. Now, shoo."

The poor man looked heartbroken, but he stumbled away after a moment.

Then, Trish linked her arm with Emma's. "He was cute, but let's go in. Tell me who you've seen, who has had way too much plastic surgery, and who is in there trying to hook up."

Emma's spirits lifted. She maneuvered Trish through the ballroom door, around the edges of the dance floor, and back to the table she'd just left. Thankfully, the loud woman who'd been at the nearby bar was nowhere to be seen—maybe she had left. Soon, Emma and Trish both had fresh wineglasses and were settled in, people-watching the crowded room.

Trish gestured with her glass. "I thought Josh Hansen was dead."

Emma almost spit her wine back into her glass as she guffawed. "What?"

"Yeah. Maybe he just faked his death. Insurance scam or something. Was it that I heard he went to jail? Gambling? Tax something?"

"I would guess prison, in that case," Emma said, snickering.

"If he comes by to try to hit on us, check for an ankle monitor."

Emma's heart squeezed in her chest. "I doubt anyone here will be hitting on me."

And I'm certainly not in the mood, she thought.

"Why not? You look smashing. Maybe Eddie Stanhope is around here somewhere…" Trish sing-songed.

"I've already seen him. He found me earlier. He's a restaurant critic now, and—"

"Oh, gosh, don't tell me. He's not the six-pack abs of your youthful dreams anymore?" Trish finished her wine and signaled a passing waiter for another.

"*Trish!*" Emma admonished. "That's not at all what I was going to say. And *I'm married*."

Something unreadable flashed across Trish's face. Emma was sure that Trish didn't like being scolded for being so superficial, but Emma didn't feel like Trish's cattiness was fair.

Trish's tone was cool when she replied. "Where is Troy, anyway? You'd think Mr. Popularity wouldn't miss this for the world."

"Yeah, about that…" Emma downed the rest of her wine just as the waiter brought Trish's second glass. Emma asked for another, and then waited until the man slipped away.

Trish was watching her intently. "About what?" Her friend's eyes were growing wider with each passing second.

Emma felt her throat start to close, so she grabbed Trish's glass and stole a sip of wine.

"I—Troy and I—I mean, you are all over the city with catering, right?"

"Right," Trish said flatly.

"And didn't you say you see Troy from time to time, at some of the parties and charity events?"

"Yep," Trish replied. "A couple times when I was subbing in back-of-house at one of the restaurants downtown."

Emma waited for Trish to elaborate, but when she didn't, Emma rushed on. "I know this seems crazy, but have you ever—"

Trish leaned forward, expectant strain on her pretty face.

"I mean, when you've seen him out without me, has there been—" Her throat still dry, Emma swallowed thickly and tried again. "The most recent place you saw him? Was it—"

"Spit it out, Emma!" Trish yelled, loud enough that people at nearby tables turned to look.

Emma leaned back, staring at her friend.

"Sorry," Trish said, her voice lowering. "I just don't get what you're asking me."

"I was gone last week, and Troy went to this fancy restaurant with another woman."

Trish huffed. "Girl, I've never worked at *Chez Fantaisie.* Why are you giving me the third degree?"

All Emma could hear in the silence that followed was her own heartbeat, as loud as a drum in her ears. She swallowed hard, trying to regain the ability to speak.

"How did you know?" Emma finally managed to whisper.

Trish wrinkled her cute button nose. "How did I know what?"

The music thumped, blasting out of the rented speakers in the corners of the room, and Emma felt every beat in her tight temples.

"I never said the name of the restaurant," Emma said, nearly shouting over the music. Then, something struck her, and a cold realization dawned. "And why didn't you ask me when you first got here where Troy was?"

Trish's eyes went impossibly wider. Her face flushed a deep beet-red, and she stammered. "E-Emma, of course you said the restaurant. And I assumed—"

Emma stood, flattening her palms on the tabletop. The room around her seemed to be spinning. "It's *you!*"

Trish stood too, stumbling back from the cocktail table. "Keep your voice *down*," Trish said, wincing. But more and more partygoers were beginning to stop and look at them.

"Why should I? *You slept with my husband*."

The dance number that had been playing cut at just that moment, sending the last four words of Emma's proclamation echoing across the ballroom. Then, the DJ's voice boomed over the speakers, not missing a beat.

"Okay, Haven High alumniiiii! It's time to slow it down with a little love song for the couples."

"*You,*" Emma repeated as she stepped back forcefully, nearly tripping on her own high heels, "betrayed me."

CHAPTER THREE

Her best friend—the *woman who Troy had been cheating with*—reached out to try to catch her. Emma jerked her arm away.

"Don't touch me. Y-y-you. *And Troy*?"

Trish blinked. She tried again to grab for Emma, and Emma saw the flash on Trish's wrist that she had missed before—a delicate silver bracelet, with a dangling charm iconic enough that, even in motion, Emma recognized the twinkling, tiny word cast in the same precious metal.

Lush.

The air-conditioned ballroom was too hot. Emma felt like her skin was on fire as anger welled up in her, and hot tears filled her eyes. "All the times Troy didn't want me to come home early from work trips—he was meeting you. He would tell me to go sightseeing, to relax, take my time. And when I came back to LA, when *we* were meeting for brunch. You buddied up with me, *knowing* what you two were doing behind my back."

Trish stammered, "E-Emma, I can explain."

Emma laughed bitterly. "Oh, I bet you can. Let's hear it."

"It just h-happened. A couple years ago, my catering business was struggling. You're right, Troy and I did meet, but it wasn't like that. Not at first. He just offered to invest. And then, we went to dinner to discuss the money. And…"

"It just kept *happening* for how long?"

Trish didn't reply, at first. Then, she raised her chin, her brown eyes flashing. "A couple years."

Emma couldn't breathe.

"You know, Emma, he deserves to be loved. Maybe if you weren't gone all the time with work." Trish's perfect features rearranged into an ugly sneer.

Anger burned hot in Emma. "Don't you *dare*."

Trish took a step toward her. Emma stepped back, looking around. Everyone surrounding them had stopped to watch the confrontation—those who weren't coupled up and swaying together on the dance floor to the crooning love song that was wafting through the ballroom.

Before Trish could say anything else, Emma turned and bolted.

***

Emma woke up several hours later, still in her dress from the reunion. Her mouth tasted sour, and she had a pounding headache that had nothing to do with the wine she'd had at the event.

Though it was the middle of the night, her racing mind revved higher as soon as her eyes opened, and she couldn't stop replaying the events of the reunion over and over.

She was definitely leaving Troy now. Her own best friend? He was the absolute *worst.* Not that Trish was any better. Emma wished a million tiny paper cuts and constant, inconvenient flat tires on both of them. Indigestion from everything except plain white bread. She hoped Trish's mascara would always clump, and that Troy's overbite would relapse, and he would have to get full-on metal braces—again.

She spent twenty minutes coming up with creative curses for the pair who had betrayed her, and then Emma resigned herself to the fact that she wouldn't be able to get any more sleep, so she got up to shower. Feeling mildly better after—and checking to make sure that she'd turned her phone back off after ordering her rideshare from the hotel—Emma padded out to the main room, raided her fridge for chocolate and Perrier, and went to the bookshelf in her living room to look for some comfort.

After several minutes of fruitless searching, she grew frustrated.

Where is that album?

She found another wedding album—hers and Troy's—and she sat down with it on the living room floor, flipping the pages and wondering where the joy of that day had gone. They'd been so young, and she'd been so optimistic. Picture after picture of them smiling, beaming at one another, dancing, feeding each other cake. Emma's stomach turned when she came to a photo of the wedding party. Trish stood beside Emma as maid of honor, her smile a mile wide.

Emma slammed the book closed, stood, and went directly to the trash compacter in the kitchen, where she dumped the whole thing in and pushed the button to crush the album the way Troy had crushed her heart.

Then, she was back to the living room to search for the only happy wedding memories that would comfort her. Emma stood on tiptoe and ran her fingers to the very top of the bookshelf, bumping a slim volume of *something.* It was too thin to be her parent's wedding album, which Emma flipped through whenever she was feeling down, but it felt familiar anyway. So, bouncing up just a tad higher, she managed to scoot the object closer. Then, she grabbed it and slid it off, dodging the few dust bunnies that rained down with it.

Emma actually smiled softly when she saw what the mystery object was. It was the portfolio she'd used to land her first position at VogueThink. Flipping through the printed and bound file, she reminisced at the creations inside. One piece in particular lifted her mood slightly—the view from her Aunt Pip's front porch. Phillipa lived in a massive old house on a bluff overlooking the sea in Haven by the Sea, Emma's hometown and where Troy's family vineyard was. It was a gorgeous view. There were nature images she'd painted over the years, as well as still-life art. The last file in the portfolio was of Troy, a portrait Emma had created using his eighth-grade school picture as a reference. Rather than a direct copy, the portrait was rendered in neon '80s-style colors. The effect was akin to pop art, and Emma loved it, regretting only the *subject*, and not the *work.*

She had made some crazy art when she'd been younger. And, looking back, she wondered if that had been the last time she'd felt truly free and happy. Before she'd been dazzled by the paycheck offered to her—and its increases—as she'd moved from art to advertising, from a lowly staff artist to the head executive of VogueThink. Now, the closest she got to inspiration was the color-coded quarterly reports and client satisfaction results. She guessed there was an art, of a sort, to managing their project tracking software, but it wasn't exactly a creative joy.

Troy had been so unhappy with her messy studio space in their first LA apartment, just a corner she'd claimed as her own and covered in drop cloths and various spattered mediums. Now, she had an entire room off the garage that was a studio—a long-neglected one.

Emma struggled to think of a recent time when he hadn't been unhappy. Had Troy been happy, back before they'd finished college? Sure, his degree in Exercise Science wasn't exactly exciting, but it had fit with his athletic pursuits, and he'd been hoping to get drafted into pro sports out of college, anyway. But that hadn't happened. His partying had led to an injury his senior year at the university, and she'd gotten the job offer at VogueThink the summer after she'd graduated. They'd rushed to get married, caught up in the novelty of moving out as an official couple, an independent team in fast-moving, shiny Los Angeles.

Where had she—they—gone wrong? Was it that she had put too much time into her career once it'd taken off at VogueThink? Was there really—as Troy had said—a lack of connection between them?

No, she thought suddenly, vehemently. *There is no excuse for what he did.*

Her heart squeezed with fresh ache, and she put the portfolio away and turned her attention to the distraction of mindless entertainment. When nothing on any of her streaming subscriptions caught her fancy, Emma decided to finally look at her missed calls.

She poured one more glass of Perrier, steeled herself, and turned her phone on. There were twelve missed calls. Six were from Troy, four from Trish, one from her mom, and one—the last one—was from her Aunt Pip. Emma didn't want to deal with her mom, and certainly never wanted to speak to her husband again, or Trish, for that matter—unless the former was through legal counsel. But Emma hadn't heard from Aunt Pip in a while, and concern for her aging aunt overrode all the emotional uproar over Troy's shenanigans.

Knowing her eighty-going-on-twenty aunt would be up this late (Emma's clock read eleven at night), Emma dialed. Pip picked up on the second ring.

"Who sent you? Who do you work for?"

Emma actually laughed, which felt like a much needed bright spot in the darkness that had been her past couple days. "Pip, you're crazy."

"Hi, kiddo. Everything okay?"

"Yeah, I'm fine," Emma lied. "I had my class reunion today."

There was silence, and then Aunt Pip sighed on the other end. "I'm not going to soft-shoe around it, Emma. Your sister called me."

Emma frowned, raising a hand to rub at her aching temple. "Yeah, Pip. About that."

Pip clicked her tongue. "Good riddance, I say."

"It's not that simple," Emma said, and Pip jumped immediately in to cut off whatever she might have said next.

"Wait, you are leaving him, yes?"

Emma felt tears well up again. Was it always going to be like this—crying at the mere mention of Troy and their wrecked relationship? "Yes," she managed to croak.

"Thank goodness you found out now instead of a year, two years, heck, ten years down the road! And *kids*. My gosh, can you imagine if you had convinced him to change his mind about having kids? This would be a whole different mess."

Emma took a deep, wavering breath and pushed her damp, blonde hair away from her hot forehead, steadying herself as much as possible. "That's true. We never even got a pet."

"See? Because deep in your heart of hearts, you knew the signs were there. Now, come to Haven by the Sea and see me."

"Morgan tried to get me to come home already, Pip. And, thankfully, the reunion committee decided to host the reunion in Los Angeles, so I avoided Haven there. I don't think I'm up for travel right now."

Emma's phone pinged with a notification, and she pulled her phone away from her ear to see an email confirmation from an airline. She switched the call to speaker and opened the alert.

"Pip, did you just send me a plane ticket?"

"Yes, now go pack. Just a couple of things—enough for a few days. Maybe a week. Heck, why don't you come stay here through the summer? I have something to discuss with you, anyway. That's the first flight out in the morning. It's a sixty-minute trip. Troy expects you to sit at home and wait for him to come back. Don't be there when he comes crawling."

"I'll think about it."

Emma was tantalized by the idea. And Pip was right—Troy followed the same pattern: storm out and come back to grovel every single time they had a blowup. Emma had never gone this long after a fight without falling for Troy's faux charm, meant to smooth over his transgressions. Empty, hollow words that never matched the recurrence of his selfish, hurtful actions. With Pip as moral support, Emma felt confident she could get past the painful first few steps of finally breaking it off with him for good.

Pip harumphed. "What is there to think about? I've actually never liked Troy. We all just tolerated him because we thought he made you happy." Pip's voice softened. "I hate it when you're unhappy." The older woman's sympathetic tone was like a gentle pat on Emma's wounded heart. "Listen. I know you're just pacing around that house, stewing over what happened. Everything there is a reminder. You want to bulldoze the whole place, right?"

"Not the *whole* place," Emma grumbled. "I might go rent someplace for a little while, just until I feel better."

"No. Come stay here at Cliffside with me for a bit. It's nothing fancy, you know, but you can nurse your broken heart here instead of all by yourself at some yuppie B and B. The cove will do you good. It's peaceful."

"Pip, not everyone who runs a B and B is a yuppie. Calm down."

Another harrumph. "You're taking at least a few days with me whether you like it or not."

At first, Pip's suggestion sounded crazy. All summer at the cove? How would she work?

Doing some mental gymnastics, and wondering how many IT favors she could call in, Emma had the faintest hope that she could figure out something. A quick call to VogueThink might even be enough to set her up to work remotely from Haven by the Sea for the whole summer. And it would occupy her to have her family around, rather than just her work colleagues and her circle of Los Angeles friends—who all happened to also be Troy's friends. Emma really had no excuse not to go back to Haven.

"You can't say no to me," Pip said evenly. "That ticket is nonrefundable." Emma pictured Pip's hot-purple glasses perched at the end of her nose as she looked sternly into the phone. She visualized Pip's silvery pixie cut. She could have placed a bet that her aunt was wearing the band T-shirts and workout leggings that Pip wore all the time (anywhere from bunco night to formal dinners). Her feisty aunt was, indeed, irresistible.

"I'd get there at breakfast," Emma said lamely, knowing it still wouldn't deter Pip.

"I'll have the bed made up before you get here. Maybe some quick brunch charcuterie.

I'll get up early to start the baked brie. Now, scoot. Get your stuff packed, and schedule a car to pick you up."

"You know I can't resist," Emma cautioned. "You or your cooking."

"Well, come on, then," Pip said.

Emma jumped into action. After a quick email to her assistant at VogueThink in which Emma asked for IT to set up a remote connection so she could work while she was there, Emma jetted to her bedroom to begin packing.

It was hard to ignore the clothes and other items of Troy's that were missing. And the empty king-sized bed that sat, neatly made, in the center of the massive master bedroom. Emma glanced over to see the slinky, red dress crumpled on the bedroom floor. She ignored it there, and then used her phone to arrange a rideshare for dawn. When she left the room, arms full of pillows and blankets, she left the puddle of red satin behind her on the carpet.

Leaving that dress behind felt like a clean start. Maybe, as in art, it was time for a do-over. A fresh start. A clean canvas.

Emma piled pillows and blankets on the sectional, creating a cozy nest that she snuggled down in, hoping elusive sleep could sneak past the events of the day and her currently racing mind.

Tomorrow, she would go to Haven by the Sea—and whatever summer there promised her.

CHAPTER FOUR

The next day dawned clear and lovely, and Emma watched the sun rise over Haven by the Sea as the small plane she was on began to circle, preparing to descend to the runway. The first golden rays sparkled over the placid waters of the cove—a wide, arcing inlet that was not often as calm as it was now, but typically crashed in frothy waves against the sheer cliffs that sheltered a half-dozen broken stretches of soft, sandy shore.

Haven by the Sea itself, the quaint little town that began at the fishing harbor where the cliffs ended, stretched back from the coast enough to form a village just large enough to be put on a map. Emma counted fishing boats dotting the dawn waters, and she would bet that the population of the quaint, picture-perfect town was only half of what it would be when all those fishermen came in for the evening—though even the resident tally when everyone was home for dinner wouldn't impress anyone from Los Angeles.

The plane bounced once, twice, three times as its wheels hit the tarmac, and Emma's already unsettled stomach did a few extra somersaults. Haven by the Sea International was aptly named—if one considered that, when Emma had been a child, a plane from Canada once had to make an emergency landing on the airfield's one commercial runway. She made a mental note to find out if the "international" had actually been added after the incident—and she actually had to stifle a smile.

There was no luggage to speak of, only the carry-on that she'd stuffed full of spring-appropriate wear, and so Emma lugged her single bag to the arrivals exit—on account of a broken wheel, which was just her luck—and hoofed it to a taxi that was idling in the passenger pickup turnoff. Inside, a grizzled man who looked to be in his sixties was dozing behind the wheel of the parked car.

Emma rapped at the passenger window.

The man startled awake, fumbling to roll down the window.

"You working?" she asked, already scanning the empty stretch of asphalt behind him for a (nonexistent) second cab.

"Yes, ma'am," he said, sitting up and rubbing at his eyes. He offered her a crooked but charming smile, and then popped the driver's side door and shifted his lanky frame out of the cab.

As he loaded her bag into the trunk and opened the back door of the cab, he said, "Sorry 'bout that. You're the first fare I've had this mornin', and I forgot my coffee."

"No problem," Emma replied, and she felt a yawn come over her. Blinking, she added, "I haven't had any, either."

The cabbie returned to the driver's seat and turned to look at her. "Name's Bill. You know where you're goin'?"

"Emma," she said, holding out her hand. "And if The Humble Pie is still around, and you know the way, I'll buy you a cup of coffee."

Bill smiled again, the expression lighting up a face that looked more like that of a seasoned sea captain than an airport taxi driver. He took her hand and shook it, and his short, bushy gray moustache danced as he spoke.

"Missy, you have got a deal."

Unlike the rest of California, Haven by the Sea didn't suffer from traumatic early-morning traffic congestion, and Emma was able to sit back and relax as they left the airport and headed for downtown. Bill turned on an old Blues station, and Emma let the smooth sound of someone else's broken heart wash over her, feeling relieved to be back in a place she felt at home.

As they crested a hill that dipped quickly on the far side into Haven by the Sea's main drag, Emma craned to catch the first glimpse of Main Street that she'd had in years. Her eyes welled a bit when she saw that it was relatively unchanged. As they glided down into town and began passing the rows of shops, she looked for her favorites.

"Mandy's Candies! Still there!" she squealed, turning as they passed to make out the sweets displayed in the window. "And the Boot Barn. And they rebuilt the gazebo by the courthouse!"

Bill chuckled. "You been here before, I guess."

"I grew up here. Well, through high school. Moved to LA, and my mom followed."

"Your dad still here, then?" Bill asked easily—but the question sent a lancing pain through Emma that she'd felt a million times.

"He passed when I was thirteen. But my aunt's still here. I used to spend a lot of time with her. She would watch me and my sister when our folks went away. But college happened, work happened, and I haven't been back in way too long."

"Went away where?" Bill scratched his moustache. Emma was actually grateful that he didn't say he was sorry about her dad—today, she couldn't take the weight of another sorry. Not from Troy, or Trish, or even a well-meaning moue of sympathy from a cab driver about her sad family past.

Emma shook her head. "Funny you ask that. I have no idea. It never seemed weird to me as a kid, but they would drop us off at her house and be away for a few weeks. Once even on Christmas. When they came back, they never talked about it. My aunt never talked about it."

"Who's your aunt?"

"Phillipa Chambers. She lives up on Cliffside." It was amusing that Bill's gruff, few-word replies and blunt questions were bringing up so much from Emma's past. A cab ride with some ghosts.

Welcome home, I guess, she mused.

Emma was surprised by Bill's indelicate answering snort. "Pip? Yeesh! I hope you're a lot nicer than that crazy gal is."

As Bill navigated the taxi into a wide U-turn on the empty street to park alongside the curb next to Haven by the Sea's best bakery, Emma laughed. "That depends. What'd she do to you?"

"Cheated me at cards at the VA poker night, that's what. I don't know how, and I can't prove it, but she cheated."

Emma felt her second smile of the day threaten to come out. "And what'd she win?"

Bill mumbled something under his breath. Emma shouldered her purse and unbuckled her seatbelt, scooting up to the space between the front two seats. "What? I didn't hear that."

"A *date*," the older man hissed. "I had to take her out to dinner."

Well, shoot. At least someone is having fun with the whole love thing, Emma thought. Her smile was now a full-blown goofy grin.

"Well, you make it sound like you had a bad time. Did you?"

After a beat, Bill answered. "No. It was actually pretty okay. We went to Rooster's Café."

Emma somehow knew he would be affronted if she laughed, so she simply let the grin break so wide across her lips that it was almost painful, holding back her laughter. Now she had something to tease Pip about.

"How do you take your coffee?" she asked Bill as she climbed out of the back of the cab.

"As black as Phillipa Chambers's heart!" he mock-roared, but he was smiling. He leaned out the open window of the cab as Emma reached the door to The Humble Pie. "Wait!"

Emma turned back to see the older man's brow furrowed, his face serious.

"I would have asked her out without the cards, you know. But it's the fact she *cheated*."

Emma's chest pinched at the word, even though it hadn't been used in the context that she'd heard it.

"All's fair in love and poker, right?" she said airily.

Bill was still grumbling when she pulled open the bakery door and slipped inside.

***

"Emma Sullivan, is that you?"

The tiny redhead behind the counter at The Humble Pie nearly vaulted over the pink Formica counter as the smell of sugar, caramel, fresh apples, and brewing coffee washed over Emma. It took her a moment to register that Hallie—Nelson, if she hadn't married since Emma had left Haven by the Sea—had used Emma's maiden name. It felt weird, but a little nice. A thrill of unexplained emotion zipped through her.

"Hallie!" Emma opened her arms in time to catch the tight hug of her old high school friend. "You're running this place? What about your mom?" Then, thinking of her own late father, Emma winced. "Sorry. I hope she's not—is she okay?"

Hallie pulled away, still smiling. She swatted Emma with the oven mitt that she had on, and a poof of flour erupted from it. "Oh, she's fine, silly. Retired. Moved to the cutest little fifty-five-plus community not far from here. I couldn't pass up taking over this sweet little kingdom." She waved her oven mitt around at the mint-green walls of The Humble Pie, which were lined with long pink counters and chrome barstools. The whole back of the store was taken up with glass display cases full of homemade pies, tarts, and other baked goods.

"So, what are you in town for?" Hallie asked, sashaying back behind the displays.

"One of your apple pies, of course," Emma said, hoping that Hallie wouldn't ask too many questions. Ones Emma didn't have the answers to—and didn't want to, just yet. "And two black coffees. To go."

Hallie busied herself with packing up the pie (crumb top, to Emma's great delight) and the coffees. She plunked the to-go cups into a cardboard drink carrier, and, after ringing Emma up, offered to help her out to the car. Just as Emma was thinking of an excuse to go it alone—after all, a walk to the car would be another chance for Hallie to ask about Troy—the bell over the door jingled, and a couple walked in.

"Thanks, I got it," Emma whispered as she balanced the coffees on top of the pink cardboard box that held the pie. Hefting both, she swerved around the newly arrived pair and put her back to the glass door at the entrance.

Pushing hard, Emma swung out onto the sidewalk—and directly into the soft-but-solid wall of another person. Stumbling back, she watched as the drink carrier tipped, wobbled—and was caught by a large, masculine hand. She clutched the pie box tightly, going statue-still. She followed the hand to an arm, and the arm to the short sleeve of a tight black T-shirt, and that sleeve up to a curl of brown hair that rested—just a tad too long, in Emma's opinion—on the collar that ringed a tanned neck.

"Excuse me. I'm so sorry!" the hand said. Er, the *man* said. And then, Emma looked at him in the face, instead of maybe, possibly, admiring just how nice the jaw that slanted from the tanned neck was.

He had slightly heavy brows that were drawn together over troubled green eyes. A strong nose, with a bit of a quirky bridge that looked as though he'd broken it a time or two. Nice lips if she thought to notice that sort of thing. And she definitely didn't.

"T-that's okay," she managed to squeak. Not a drop of her coffee had spilled, but she looked at his chest—*across* his chest—to see that he held the lid to a cup of coffee in his free hand. The rest of the cup was on the front of his shirt and all over the sidewalk, the cup rolling, the milky brew spreading over the cement.

"Oh no." She started to kneel to clean up the spill. But she had nothing in her hands to clean up with. She left the man standing there, holding her drink carrier with the two coffees in it, as she whisked the pie box out from underneath it. Flustered, she just set the bakery box on top of the puddle.

Then, mortified at the un-solution, she took the coffees from him, put them back on the pie box, and picked up the box—which was now soaked in coffee.

The man blinked at her. "Are you okay?"

"Nope!" Emma heard from behind her. "She's Pip Chambers's niece!"

Emma wanted to sink into the sidewalk.

Shut up, Bill.

"Oh. The Victorian on Cliffside. I'm Hudson," Nice Lips said. He was still holding the coffee cup lid, but he thrust out his free hand as though he was not also covered in the fallout of her clumsiness. "I own the new antique shop."

Emma lifted the soggy box in response to his offered handshake. "Sorry. I've got to go." She turned on her heel and marched back to Bill's cab. She studiously avoided looking back at where Hudson was standing as she plunked the pie onto the seat beside her, handed Bill his coffee, and barked, "Drive."

Bill just nodded, put the cab into drive, and pulled back out onto Main.

"He's a real nice guy, that fella you just threw coffee on," Bill said evenly.

Oh my gosh, I left him covered in coffee. I didn't even help him clean up!

Emma sank down into the backseat, even more mortified. She didn't realize until they were at Pip's that Bill hadn't even had to ask her directions to the house. He stopped the cab just short of Pip's front porch, unloaded Emma's bag, refused to take any money from her, and gave her a brief but warm hug before quickly backing out of the long, gravel drive.

Emma was standing in the driveway holding her coffee cup when Pip came out, wearing tuxedo trousers, a Led Zeppelin tee, and pair of red suspenders. She was smoking a cigar.

"Hey, kiddo!" her aunt yelled across the driveway. "Was that Bill? How was your trip?"

She clutched the coffee cup tighter. Unexpectedly, she felt a sense of overwhelming sadness wash over her, and the adrenaline that had fueled her since the fight with Troy seemed to leave her all at once, underlining how she'd been running on fumes for days. Her shoulders slumped, her throat burned, and all she wanted was to rush into her aunt's arms and spill all the details of what a rollercoaster things had been, all of her current pain and sorrow—not to mention embarrassment.

Emma knew she didn't have to put on a brave face, but she'd been doing it for so long that it was almost automatic. Steadying her swirling thoughts, Emma plastered on a smile and started toward the porch, hoping Pip couldn't see through to the tears that she was barely holding back.

CHAPTER FIVE

"Oh, it's okay. The outside is a mess, but all is actually fine inside. A metaphor for life if I ever heard one." As she spoke, Pip eyed Emma—but Emma avoided her gaze.

Emma watched Pip lift the sugar-dusted apple pie out of the mushy Humble Pie box, relieved to see that the pie itself was unharmed. Pip set it on the massive island that centered the eat-in kitchen, and set about rummaging through cabinets. "I've got a pie stand in here somewhere..."

A few crashes and bangs later, Pip came up with a deep blue, beaded glass pie stand, smiling triumphantly. The pie was balanced on it and covered with a matching top, protected from any invaders—or Emma's next social *faux pas*.

It was comforting being in the old house again, the smells of the aging wood and plaster reminding Emma of childhood. And her aunt was as unchanged as the house—oh, perhaps a little older, but still as warm and welcoming (and quirky) as Cliffside itself. She had hugged Emma silly on arrival, offered her a cigar (which she had declined), and brought her inside without one mention of Troy, which Emma was thankful for.

Now, Emma took in the full effect of Aunt Phillipa. The Led Zeppelin tee, suspenders, and tuxedo pants were complimented by a pair of chunky black boots that added at least three inches to Pip's compact height. Her icy silver hair was cut in a pixie that was wildly tousled above her ears, just a little longer than she normally wore it.

Emma sipped a fresh cup of coffee, her first to-go cup from the bakery now empty and sitting in Pip's garbage can—down in the dumps, a place Emma could identify with. "Well, the pie might be saved, but nothing's going to save me from all of Haven by the Sea now knowing that Emma Sullivan's back in town—and weirder than ever!"

Pip *tsked* as she retrieved two dinner plates from another cupboard and rejoined Emma at the marble island, sliding onto a creaky stool next to her. "Who cares if they think you're weird. Weird is cool. Look at me. I'm so weird, and have been for so long, that I think every busybody in town has just circled back to considering me normal."

Emma took an offered plate from Pip and stood to begin filling it with food from the myriad dishes spread out over the island. Into varying sizes of sturdy white casserole dishes emblazoned with delicate blue flowers, Pip had baked and layered and piled a smorgasbord of brunch delicacies. Way too much for two people, but plenty to comfort Emma's lovesick, homesick, now socially pariah-ed heart.

Baked brie and apricot jam with buttery, paper-thin almond and ginger crackers. A quiche with swirls of spinach and diced ham that was surrounded by toast points. Goat cheese and cold roasted beets, drizzled with balsamic syrup and sparkling with coarse salt. Cinnamon pecan rolls. A tart mixture of olives, pickled turnips, mini kosher dills, and cocktail onions. Emma's mouth watered as she took some of each.

When her plate was full, and as she dished up food for Pip, Emma looked around the kitchen. It had been kept up in all the years that she had been gone, probably owing to the fact that her aunt loved to cook. But the view out the kitchen door, into the once-regal formal living room…

"Pip, is Louise still coming in to keep up the housework?" Of course, the housekeeper had been in her fifties even back when Emma had been coming to Cliffside as a child. But it was as good an opener as any.

"Oh, heavens, no," Pip answered, spearing a beet, and chewing thoughtfully. "She retired years ago. To this nice little fifty-five plus place nearby. Part of why this place is such a disaster."

"Oh. Wonder if it's the same place Hallie's mom went."

"Yep. Carol Nelson was the first of us to go there."

Something about that wording—*first of us*—sent up Emma's antenna. But she didn't push for details. "I could help clean the house up a bit while I'm here. If it'll help you once I'm gone."

Pip's expression changed, and she looked almost pained for a moment. Then, squaring her shoulders, she set her fork down and patted the stool next to her. Emma returned to the seat, ignoring her own food for the moment.

"Dear, I have a confession to make." Pip's hands fluttered against the marble island. "I asked you here for a reason. I mean a different reason, aside from helping you escape from the obvious, annoying grovel-fest that Troy, the subadult boy, would be laying on you right about now."

Emma reached up and covered Pip's hands with her own. Her aunt's skin felt so delicate, her fingers not as strong as Emma had once thought them. And her own hands, well, they looked strangely adult next to her aunt's. It was a stark reminder that time hadn't slowed down, not when Emma had been away in Los Angeles, and not here in little Haven by the Sea. She waited for Pip to continue.

"Look, this house is massive. Way too big for me. The porch is sagging, the floors are coming up, and the pipes cry like teenagers cut off from the interwebs."

"The what?" Emma giggled.

"The tickler tocks. The myfaces. Instagramps—never quite figured that one out, seems lots of youngsters in bikinis, dragging their boyfriends down the beach or across rope bridges." As Emma tried to keep a straight face, Pip confidently clarified, "You know, the friends you keep in your phone."

Emma just nodded and thought of her phone, which she had let die completely. Work had orders to email her if they needed her, with a strict window of reply hours that ensured she wouldn't spend her whole trip buried in her inbox. Being so off the radar was actually pretty freeing. She hadn't been this detached from work and the world in years.

Pip's hands curled under Emma's. "I have really been struggling with the upkeep over the past couple years. I"—Pip broke off and looked down at the floor—"I've closed up most of the house. I've sort of been living in just a few of the rooms."

"Pip!" Emma couldn't contain her shock. What she'd seen of the house as she'd come through the foyer, past the living room, and into the kitchen hadn't seemed that bad. What Pip was describing was serious disrepair.

"Truthfully, the rest is going to rot," Pip said bluntly. "The old girl has got good bones, but the flesh on her is well over a hundred years old. What do you expect?" She drew her hands out from under Emma's and resumed eating, waving with her free hand as if to dismiss her earlier discomfort.

"What about Morgan? She hasn't been around to help?" Emma picked up her own fork and began to eat, making a mental note to call her sister from Pip's landline and tell her she'd arrived safely in town.

"You know she's busy with the kids. And Eric. And did you know the new dog had puppies last month?"

"She told me." Emma marveled at how her sister could keep up with it all. A hectic day at the office seemed like a cakewalk in comparison. "I don't know how she can handle another being to care for in that house."

Pip smiled cheekily. "Oh, I expect she'll manage it. But be warned—she might rope you into volunteering with her at the animal rescue where mama woof came from."

Emma smiled into her coffee as she took another sip. "Pip. She's really dedicated to that! Don't make fun."

"Yes, she is. One of these unused rooms has about twenty cases of canned dog food in it from shelter overflow. I expect Morgan'll always need extra storage for her cause, so when you inherit this house, I hope you still let her stash her goodies here."

Emma took another, more careful sip of her coffee. "When I inherit? Stop it. You're going to live forever."

"No one does, dear. But I'm not talking about when I shuffle off this mortal coil. I'm talking about right now. I'm moving to Carmel." Pip rushed on before the full impact of her words hit Emma. "I put in a bid on the best unit they have at that fifty-five-plus place. Carol and Louise love it there. It's gorgeous; all the villas are on the lakefront. It's practically a resort. They have game nights, dancing, food truck Fridays. There is a resident concierge desk, and they will bring you things from the community grocery, even firewood for your fireplace. People will be waiting on *me* for a change. No renovations or upkeep to manage, and Bill Hawkins already has a place of his own there. Easier for me to chase him if he's just a few houses down."

Emma nodded, still not quite getting where she fit in with Pip's retirement plan. "Well, I'm happy if you are, Pip."

"Gosh, you're taking this so well. This big old house is just a pain in my ass. I was going to sell it way under value just to get rid of it, but I don't need the money, and it's such a dump anyway. So I'm just going to give it to you."

The intention hit. Emma shook her head, laughing a short, mirthless laugh. "What would I do with the place? I don't know the first thing about renovating a house, or managing a renovation if I hired out. I don't even live here!"

Pip mimicked Emma's laugh, but hers was genuine. "You'll figure it out. I was going to call you about it next week, after I'd already moved out—I figured it would be less hectic if I got my own things out to the new house before I handed over Cliffside to you. But Troy went ahead and showed his true colors, and—if there is a silver lining to his black deed—that made it easy for me to tell you now. It worked out. You can move here. And you can help me pack. The paperwork is at my lawyer's for the deed change and property transfer. The old place is your blessing and problem now."

With a wink, Pip dug enthusiastically into her quiche.

"No way," Emma sputtered. "Pip, there's no way I could."

Inside, Emma's heart beat a mile a minute. Half of her was terrified at what Pip was suggesting—take over Cliffside? That meant leaving everything in Los Angeles.

The other half of her was—surprisingly—giddy at the thought. This house had no pool to remind her of unneeded excess, no angular, modern architecture that made it feel more like an art museum than a home, no smoggy commutes, and none of the emotional specters of her failed marriage.

Emma felt tears well in her eyes. "Why do you want to give me Cliffside? You could sell it, bank the money, for whatever it's worth, and not be bothered."

"Money? What do I want money for? I'm a spinster who invested well, so hush."

As Emma started to protest her aunt's slightly unflattering classification, Pip clicked her tongue to interrupt.

"You could be happy here again," Pip said gently, setting down her fork. "I would love to see that. The old girl needs work, and, honey, so do you. Maybe you can fix each other up." Her aunt's beseeching blue eyes were full of concern, and that hit Emma right in the heart. She felt a swell of gratitude at the generosity of Pip's offer, and at the knowledge that Pip was worried for her.

Morgan had coerced Emma into the reunion, but the reality talks—splitting assets and name changes and what to tell everyone at family get-togethers—would come soon with the other women in her life. Emma knew everyone was worried about her, but she had managed to avoid painful, in-depth conversations with her mom and sister so far. But there was no avoiding Pip's worry in this precise moment.

Emma felt as though an immense weight had settled on her shoulders, and fear stabbed through her. It was too much, too fast. She couldn't handle all this change in the span of a few short days. She almost felt dizzy at the possibility, scared of taking a leap into something so huge too fast. What if she did get back together with Troy (though the little voice in her head screamed in protest every time the thought crossed her mind)? Emma knew she couldn't say yes to taking the house—not without giving it some serious thought.

"I-I'm not sure. Can I sleep on it?"

Pip nodded. "Of course." The older woman picked up her fork and wagged it at Emma. "But your sister already turned down part ownership, so if you leave me high and dry, I'll have to part the whole house out to that cute new antiques guy in town."

Emma laughed, swiping at the tears that still clouded her eyes. "I have nothing to say about *that*."

Pip gave her knee a squeeze. "Let's talk about something else, then. Let's forget houses and garbage-level men for the rest of the day."

"Ok, Pip. I'll try," Emma promised.

They resumed eating and chatting about the things that Emma had missed over the past few years in Haven, and Emma laughed and smiled and ate way too much brie as her aunt filled her in. And when they were bursting full with the meal Pip had prepared, they each still devoured a slice of the apple pie.

But under all the merriment, Emma's stomach churned. She couldn't possibly take over Cliffside. Though the wooden rafters and wainscoted walls reminded her of happier times, how in the world could she just relocate her entire life back to Haven?

***

That afternoon, after a long nap that she hadn't intended to take, Emma trotted drowsily down one of the meandering hallways that led from the guest wing to the formal living room. As she passed each closed bedroom door—five in total—she padded over to try the doorknobs. As Pip had said, each was locked. It seemed the only room open in the entire wing was the one that Emma was staying in.

She reached the living room but found no one there. The front bay window of the formal living room looked out over the neglected front lawn of Cliffside, and Emma stood a moment, heedless of her puppy-print pajama pants and tank top, just staring out at the waist-high grass. Many a summer she'd spent running the dips and rises of the land surrounding Pip's sprawling Victorian with her sister, neither of them concerned about why their parents had left them in Pip's care or where they went on their mysterious trips. But Bill's innocent question had made Emma start to wonder…

"Oh! You're up."

Pip's voice broke into Emma's wandering thoughts. She turned to find her aunt in the high, arching doorway between the kitchen and the formal living room. Pip's arms were piled high with hat boxes of all sizes.

"Hey. Yeah, guess I needed sleep more than I thought. Didn't get much last night."

Pip clicked her tongue in sympathy and trudged toward Emma. Emma met her halfway to the bay window, relieving her of three round, dusty boxes. Motes rose from the embossed surfaces, causing Emma to cough and wave at the cloud of debris, trying to balance the hat boxes and catch some fresh air.

"Careful," Pip joked. "None of them have pies in them, but there's glass in a few of these."

"Ha ha," Emma deadpanned, following her aunt to the heavy, claw-footed coffee table that sat in the middle of the living room. They set down the hat boxes, and Pip opened one of the two she'd carried.

Inside the box were dress-up clothes that Emma remembered vividly from her childhood. She gasped, reaching out to touch the pile of velvets and laces and fluffy, wispy tulle. The dress-up trunk had lived in Morgan's room here at Cliffside, and it had overflowed with old Halloween costumes, fancy thrift-store finds, and even a handful of prop and clothing castoffs from the Haven by the Sea Playhouse, where Pip had volunteered years back.

"Is this all there is left?" Emma asked a little sadly.

"Most of these are the playthings from the trunk," Pip said. "Two of the boxes have vintage Christmas ornaments. That's the glass I wanted to be careful of. I figured, while I'm here, I might as well help clear as much as I can while I pack up the necessities. Leave you to deal with as little accumulation as possible."

Emma looked up, picturing the attic that ran the full length and width of Cliffside's uppermost floor. "What else is up there? You never let us go up when we were little."

"Well, lots, to be honest. Forty years in a house, you collect a lifetime supply of stuff and things."

The sting in her eyes caught Emma by surprise. She reached up and swiped at her damp lashes with the back of a hand.

Must be the dust.

"Yeah, I always wanted to be able to say that. Have a place like this—full of family, a dog, kids running around upstairs so loud that it sounds—"

"Like they're coming through the ceiling?" Pip finished.

Emma laughed. "How many times did you have to tell us to slow down and walk when we were on the second floor?"

"Countless." Pip snaked an arm around Emma's waist and drew her in close.

Emma tilted her head to the side, resting her cheek on top of her aunt's head. "Pip, things are a mess. I wish things were simple again, the way they were when I was with you all those summers."

Pip heaved a big sigh, big enough that Emma felt her side move with the effort. "You see those years through rose-colored glasses, kiddo. Things were a hot mess back then, too. But you were loved. And Morgan was loved. Your mom, your dad. We all loved each other fiercely."

They stood there, staring down at the open box for a few minutes. Emma noticed that the lace on one of the dresses was ragged, disintegrating with age and the likely poor storage conditions of the attic. Emma imagined all the other boxes stuffed up in the musty space, forgotten through the damp winters and seaside summers, and all the closed-up rooms that housed the various things that Pip had gathered over the years. Looking around the living room, Emma could see that the wallpaper was peeling, the ceilings bore suspicious little dark spots in places, and the carpets were threadbare—the worn places covered strategically with furniture, but noticeable if you knew where to look. Cliffside was fading, just like the idyllic days of Emma's childhood.

And Troy had betrayed the last sliver of youthful ideation that Emma had held onto. All those years growing up together. All those years where, now looking back, she could see that *she* had been the only one doing the growing up. He had stayed that golden, popular boy, immune to the consequences of his own actions, floating through life on the benevolence that was afforded him because of his good looks and wealth. But the shine was off, for Emma. Maybe that was why he'd cheated with Trish—maybe Trish still saw him the way he wanted to be seen.

It wasn't fair, but it was the reality of things. Emma could now either stay here at Cliffside, stewing in her pain, or become the bitter divorcee throwing herself into her work back in the city. At least in Los Angeles, she would have the office to escape to.

She'd have to tell Pip no. Or just accept the house and sell it. But what would it be like with someone else living here? Would they simply tear the house down, leaving no trace of the joy that had once dwelled here?

"What's going on in that head of yours?" Pip asked.

"Nothing." Emma sighed. "Let's sort all this stuff out, and you can show me what else you need help with."

Emma had made up her mind. Tomorrow, she would tell Pip that she was turning down the house.

CHAPTER SIX

"I'll be back after dark! You sure you'll be okay?"

Emma craned her neck back to try to see up the ladder to the attic, where Pip had disappeared for about the hundredth time. Emma's back and shoulders ached from repeated trips up that cursed, rickety ladder, and so she stayed sitting firmly on the floor of the second story, dreading having to climb up even one more time. She couldn't for the life of her imagine now why she had been so eager to go up into the attic as a child. She was dirty, sweaty, and she smelled like mothballs from her attic adventure.

It had been two hours of musty, dusty work, clearing out the absolute layers of life that existed in the attic. It was like counting the rings on a tree to determine its age—only less fresh sawdust smell and wood sap, and more old newspapers, an abundance of bowling shoes, and more cobwebs than Emma was comfortable with.

Pip's head appeared in the ladder frame in the ceiling. "Of course. Sheesh. I've been here all this time without you, I can survive a few evening hours." Then, she disappeared back into the attic.

"Don't use the propane lantern up there!" Emma yelled as she got to her feet from her cross-legged position.

"Yes, auntie!" Pip yelled back. "Keys are in the kitchen, hanging by the sink!"

Emma rolled her eyes and dusted off her pajama pants. It didn't take her long to change back into the jeans and T-shirt she'd worn on the plane that morning, and before she breezed out the door, she snagged the keys that Pip had mentioned.

Dusk was falling over Cliffside, and the sharp salt smell of the ocean hit Emma as she jogged down the sagging front steps, her sneakers crunching on the thin gravel path through the front yard. Pip's truck was parked in the same spot it had always been—and, in fact, the old seventies Ford was the same exact vehicle, too. Emma ran a hand over its pale blue and white paint job, loving even the rough touch of rust that she could feel at the edge of the bed.

The truck started up strongly on the first try, and Emma flipped on the headlights, surprised by the brightness of the beams that jumped to life. She guessed they would come in handy for the misty Haven by the Sea mornings, when the fog rolled in from the ocean and covered everything in a wet, velvety blanket of seriously low visibility. More than once as a teenager, Emma had felt she was taking her life in her hands driving the curving roads in and around Haven by the Sea on foggy nights.

She checked her watch—just about half an hour before she'd promised Morgan she'd come by. Emma eased the old pickup down the winding road to the two-lane that led back to town, and resolved to enjoy the fifteen-minute drive to her sister's.

She managed not to worry over her crumbling life for ten of those fifteen minutes, which she took as a win. Before she knew it, she was turning into the driveway of Morgan's low, expansive ranch-style house, the brick painted over in a cheerful yellow, the red front door festooned with some floral arrangement that made sure anyone visiting knew the season. This time, it was lilies and lavender and plastic glitter letters that spelled out, "Hello, Spring!"

Emma knocked. She felt a little weird doing so, but since the youngest of Morgan's children had started walking a few months ago, Emma didn't want to risk a loose toddler—even if the neighborhood streets of Haven by the Sea proper were far from heavily trafficked.

The door opened, and there was a child there—but instead of Richie, resident drooler, knee-hugger, and stealer of hearts, Morgan's oldest daughter stood there, pouting.

Emma frowned. "Tilly, what's wrong?"

The girl pouted deeper, almost comically, and threw a look over her shoulder that was much more teenage level than her actual ten years on Earth would explain. "Mom says you're only here to visit, and that you said that I wasn't allowed to come back with you to Los Angeles." Her niece crossed her arms over her chest, tossing back long, dishwater blonde hair that was so like her mother's that Emma had childhood flashbacks.

"Well..." she began carefully, trying to calculate quickly what Morgan was up against. A ten-year-old who had a house full of three other siblings, a mom, a dad, and a herd of dogs—while her aunt had a big, fairly empty house with a pool and no chaos included.

Tilly looked at Emma expectantly.

Emma stepped inside, closed the door behind her, and started to follow the sound of dishes clanking and children laughing in the kitchen of the Taylor household. Tilly wandered beside her, still waiting, it seemed.

"You see, Tilly, I'm going to be here for longer than just a quick visit. Like, a couple weeks. I'm going to help Great-Aunt Pip pack her things up at Cliffside."

"Pack up! Where's she going?" Tilly's eyes widened.

"Yes, where is Pip going?" Morgan's voice held a note of surprise as Emma arrived in the kitchen with Tilly. But Emma instantly recognized it as false.

The kitchen, a modest-sized room, was open to a sunken family room, where two other Taylor offspring sat with Emma's brother-in-law, Eric. Moira was happily playing with a pile of construction bricks at Eric's feet, next to the sectional, her four-year-old face alight with glee. Seven-year-old Daniel was hunched in concentration next to his dad while they both played a racing game that flashed across the big-screen TV.

Emma walked past Richie, who was sitting in his high chair methodically picking cooked peas up one by one and eating them, and kissed her youngest nephew on his soft, downy hair.

"Pip wants me to move into Cliffside—no, *own* Cliffside. Both," Emma said to her sister as she set down the bottle of wine she'd brought from the cellar of Cliffside. "And don't fake like you didn't know."

Morgan opened her mouth, and then closed it, and then opened it again as if to explain. Finally, she said, "She offered to split it between us, but really, I can't handle coordinating a renovation right now. Or the responsibility of a second house." Morgan winced. "You're not mad, are you?"

Emma held up a hand. "No. I mean, you could have called me. But I don't have the energy to talk about major life changes any more today."

"So really no Los Angeles?" Tilly whined.

Morgan, her back to the room, said over her shoulder, "You can go, Tils. It's only a five-day walk if you don't sleep."

Tilly huffed, rolled her eyes, and stomped to a set of sliding glass doors that led to the backyard. "I'm going to the trampoline," she said. "The unglamorous, unfamous, boring old trampoline that everyone else has, too."

With a dramatic turn, Tilly took herself to the backyard, only looking back twice to see if they were watching her.

"Well, that happened," Emma said, holding back laughter.

"She'll get over it," Eric said, his eyes glued to the screen. "And hi, Ems. You need me to have a *talk* with Troy?" As he spoke, Eric jabbed at buttons and levers on his controller, never looking away from the video game.

"I'm good," she replied, amused by how much Eric and Daniel looked alike—same thick, brown hair, same brown eyes, everything the same, right down to the backward hats they both wore. "I think my lawyer is meaner than you are."

Eric shrugged, a smile tipping up his lips. "Be a shame if his daddy's vineyard suddenly lost water service for a couple weeks. It's spring, y'know."

"I saw on the door," Emma joked back. "But don't abuse your city council position. I promise I got this."

Eric saluted her without making eye contact, and Emma saw Morgan roll *her* eyes as she

turned from the sink, where she'd been peeling a pile of potatoes. Morgan dried her hands on a dishtowel that was hanging on the stove handle and gathered Emma into a long, comforting hug. Emma sunk in, breathed out, and said a silent thankful prayer for her steady, intuitive sister. They broke apart and smiled at one another.

"You know, I won't tell you what to do about Pip and all that, but I would love to have you close again." Emma didn't miss the worry in her sister's eyes, and she knew that Morgan must be thinking of Troy and the real reason that Emma had fled back home. But Morgan wouldn't bring it up. Not like Eric had. Not unless Emma did first. And Emma hadn't been exaggerating—between the flight, the cab ride to Cliffside and the great bulldozing of Mr. Hot Antique Store, the attic cleaning, and the general emotional strain of the past few days, Emma was done talking.

"Can we just eat a lot of food and watch "The Golden Girls" until you feel like kicking me out?"

Morgan nodded. "Of course, honey. Once this is all done, I'll put everything out family-style, and the rest of these heathens can fend for themselves. We'll use the TV on the lanai."

Just then, with a sharp bark, a three-legged Golden Retriever came bounding into the kitchen from the hallway that jutted off the back of the living room, barreling straight for Emma. Behind him, two cats gave chase, each splitting off in different directions to bounce like ping-pong balls off the sectional and TV stand. The dog skidded to a stop just at the step up to the kitchen level.

Emma went down to him, sitting on the carpeted step-down and rubbing the silky ears of the pup. "Wheatie, you're a sweetie. Yes, you are. Who is the best pirate dog in all of California? You arrrrre." When Emma hit the right spot behind Wheatie's ears, he leaned heavily into her right hand, his face full of doggie joy.

"Watch the corner!" Daniel shouted at the TV, loud enough that Wheatie startled, turned two hopping little circles, and took off for the back hallway where he'd come from. Both cats gave chase once more. Moira squealed in delight, smashed the construction brick creation she'd been making, and shouted, "*You gotta be kitten me!*"

Emma burst out laughing.

"She loves your commercial, Aunt Emma," Daniel said, laughing. "She watches it every morning after breakfast."

After a pause where she seemed to be considering her options, Moira began to rebuild her toy creation patiently.

"Good job, pumpkin," Eric cooed, looking doe-eyed down at his daughter.

"Four kids, three dogs, two cats, one husband," Emma teased, looking over her shoulder at Morgan, who had returned to the sink. "Where are the other two dogs?"

"Beast is at the vet's for a torn dewclaw—horsing around and trying to get up on the trampoline with the kids. A Great Dane! Can you imagine?"

Emma couldn't.

"And the newest pup, Muffin, is in the garage with her puppies. Eric and the kids built a virtual Taj Mahal out there for her and the new babies."

"So it's not just three dogs anymore," Emma teased.

"The more, the merrier," Morgan said, pointing her potato peeler at Emma.

"Yeah, yeah," Emma said, feeling warm inside at being amid the hustle and bustle of her sister's family. It was so different from Emma's life in LA, but—it was nice. And she had thought, at one point, that she and Troy would reach a place where they would start a family.

"Get up here and chop potatoes," Morgan said when the oven started beeping. "I'll put in the meatloaf, and we can go start up our show."

Emma stood and went to wash her hands in the sink, the noise of the living room behind her blending with the rush of water.

Would it be so bad at Cliffside if Emma could be close to Morgan and her family again?

***

It was after midnight when Emma rolled up the drive to Pip's, full and as content as she had been in a long while. She crept back into the house as quietly as one could across hundred-year-old hardwood, and she found a light burning in the kitchen still. The single hanging can light that had been left on over the island shone on a note in Pip's handwriting.

Gone to bed. Got to make a trip to the new house bright and early, but you sleep in. Leftover brunch is in the fridge. I found more of your old stuff and left a box in the living room for tomorrow. Love you.

Emma flipped the note over, wrote a quick one back that said thanks for the loan of the truck, and left a picture that Tilly had drawn for Pip—after, of course, Tilly had decided not to walk to Los Angeles—on the island along with the car keys. Then, it was tiptoe to her own room, slip back into her pajamas, and she was just about asleep in the huge four-poster feather bed when her phone lit up on the massive matching nightstand.

Shoot. She'd forgotten to turn her phone off after driving home—Morgan had insisted she switch it on when she'd left their house, and that Emma would text when she arrived back at Cliffside. Which she'd done, like a good sister. And then forgotten about, promptly. She pushed up on her elbows and leaned over the side of the bed, looking at the call screen.

Her blood practically froze in her veins. And even though she'd promised herself that she wouldn't, she answered the call.

"What do you want?"

"Babe, thank God. I've been worried sick." Troy's tone would have given maple syrup a strong case of diabetes.

"About what? The property split or what you're going to tell your parents when they ask why we're divorcing?"

Over the line, she heard him suck a breath through his teeth. "Babe,"—Emma ground her teeth at the repetition of the pet name, something she'd once found endearing but was now just as repulsive as the thought of what he'd done to her—"you can't be serious. When are you coming home? My therapist says we need to talk this out together."

"*We* need to talk? I don't need to talk to you or with you about anything. You skipped the conversation with me about how you and my *best friend* were hooking up, so I've decided that I'm going to skip all future conversation with you unless it's through my very capable, very aggressive divorce lawyer. "

There was dead silence on the other end of the line. His reply was small, and shocked, and Emma felt a thrill of triumph to find that she didn't feel at all guilty—as though all the power that Troy had held over her since their youth had evaporated. It was his fault. He had made this choice for both of them, and the only reason he was upset now was because he'd been caught, and because he'd suffer some kind of fallout for the first time in his adult life.

"I thought we could work this out," he said, his voice wavering.

"You thought wrong," she retorted flatly.

He cleared his throat. "Tell me what I can do, Ems. Do you know what it will look like if you leave me? I can't—just tell me what I have to do to get you to come home."

"I am home, Troy." Then, before he could reply, Emma hung up, switched her phone off, and slid it back onto the nightstand.

Maybe she would wait to decide on Cliffside. She didn't have to tell Pip her final decision *tomorrow.*

Emma nestled into the massive four-poster bed, the sound of the waves outside her window rhythmic and soothing.

Within minutes, she was deeply asleep.

CHAPTER SEVEN

The next day found Emma debating anew what to do about Cliffside. She sat at the kitchen island, her laptop open, sorting work emails and thinking about the tea room in the opposite wing from the downstairs bedrooms—and how it would make the perfect office space. She'd always loved it as a child, and Pip had always left it set up as though a real tea party could spring up at any moment. Emma wondered if the doors in that wing of Cliffside would be locked as well, the airy, high-ceilinged rooms that she and Morgan played hide and seek in now shuttered against the coastal light.

The light always came in just perfectly in the morning, and Emma could imagine sitting in the octagonal space with soft, cream canvas curtains billowing at the windows, the sun hitting the cream-colored tea rose wallpaper in a way that made the whole place full of soft, diffuse warmth. The bookcases in there were perfect, if she recalled correctly, and she would bring down that monstrous mahogany desk from the upstairs landing to replace the dining table, and—

Her phone rang, and her stomach twisted. But the ringtone wasn't her personal one. Relieved that it was only work calling, Emma answered on the second wave of classical music.

"Adams," she greeted.

"Emma, oh, so glad I caught you."

"Mrs. Flynn, what can I do for you?" Emma fought to keep her tone neutral—though the CEO of VogueThink Marketing was always pleasant enough, Emma had come to expect a major headache whenever the woman called. Inevitably, it was always for some task that Emma didn't want to do—and was often not even in her job description. Janice Flynn still had it locked into her head that Emma was the low-level starving artist of years back.

"Please, Mrs. Flynn? It's *Janice*."

"Janice," Emma ground out. "I'm out of town…"

"Oh, I know, dear, I saw your note on the meetings schedule. I wondered of you would do me the teeniest, tiniest favor. I mean, I know you're on vacation right now—"

"Nope, I'm working," Emma corrected, "just remotely. I actually assigned next month's deliverables to the team leads just about an hour ago. Next, I'll be looking at the budget in the SudsBros file."

"Splendid. Then you have access to your drawsuite?"

Emma paused halfway, picking up her coffee cup, staring at her phone, which was lying on the island, speaker on. "My design software? Yes…"

"My grandson's birthday is in two weeks, and my daughter can't find any invitations that she likes. So she's having some custom printed, but she needs the design, understand?"

"Janice, we have staff designers that can help you with that if you—"

"You don't want to help me? It's a simple task. I'll send you over the pictures my daughter found on the internet. You should just be able to copy those."

Headache time. It wasn't even noon.

"Does your daughter have the rights to those images?" Emma asked, already knowing the answer.

Janice huffed again. "If you don't want to help, just say so. As you pointed out, we have staff designers. I can certainly find one of those who is grateful for their job. I came to you because I thought you were an *artist*, Mrs. Adams."

Emma's ears began to warm. She had been—many years ago. But when she thought about it now, Emma *knew* she wasn't an artist in any real sense of the word anymore. What she was instead was a corporate cog, part of a machine that pumped out catchphrases and cute pet videos and waited for things to go viral to determine their value and whether they could be reproduced for bigger, better profit. That wasn't art. It was artifice.

And there was something in Janice Flynn's tone that reminded Emma exactly of how Troy had spoken to her last night—*I thought we could work this out.* Like Emma was just a means to an end, someone who should get with the program and get out of the way of what everyone else wanted, regardless of how it affected her. Troy and his wandering eye. Janice Flynn and her complete lack of respect for anyone around her.

"No, you came to me because I'm nice enough to put up with your pressuring use of employee time for personal projects, Janice." It was out before Emma could control it—and once it was, Emma actually raised a hand to her mouth, shock silencing her.

"What did you just say to me?" Janice's previous tone, fake and cheery, was dropped in favor of cold, sharp anger.

"No. I'm not going to do your invitations," Emma asserted.

"Well, I hope you have a savings account, Mrs. Adams, or that your husband's family money will get you through life, because marketing might seem big, but it's a very small world at the top. You'll never work in this indus—"

Whether it was panic or her own anger or simply the fact that Emma had reached the end of her rope in multiple facets of her life, she took as deep a breath as she could and blurted, "You know what? I quit."

Then, she hung up the phone on Janice Flynn as fast as she had on her soon-to-be-ex-husband the previous night. It was getting to be a habit—a good one or a bad one, Emma couldn't decide. But along with the second hang up came the same feeling that Emma had when she'd gussied up the guts for the first. Elation. Freedom. The sensation as if a very heavy burden had been lifted.

Before Janice could recover and call her back, Emma powered down her phone. She shut her laptop, got up from the island, and went to the living room to pace.

Oh my gosh. Oh, my gosh. Oh, my gosh.

What had she done? She needed her job. The house in LA. Her car. She had worked and sacrificed and wasted too much time to-to-to…

To end up unhappy.

It hit her like a ton of bricks. She'd been reluctant to get out of the comfy featherbed this morning, dreading doing any work. Of course, her first thought had been that she was just loath to try to summon any focus while in Haven by the Sea because of its vacation-like vibes, but the real truth of the matter was that she was dreading work itself. The drudgery. The sameness. The creative stagnation that had crept over her during the past years and ensured that she was, artistically, as flexible as the layers of routine that had cemented her into her current life, her current job, her typically fast-paced, empty existence. No slowdown. No stopping to appreciate the simple things. No joy—at least, nothing that brought *her* joy.

Back and forth Emma paced, back and forth, until she was worried she'd wear new paths in the fraying carpet. Her world was spinning out of control, and yet she felt oddly at peace. So what if she wasn't at VogueThink anymore? Did she really need LA and the smog and the traffic and the gated house? Did she really need to spend her life selling the same thing to people over and over—emotionless, save the drive it took to apply the psychology of the sale?

Out of the corner of her eye, Emma spied the box that Pip had mentioned in her note—a beat-up cardboard affair that showed no outward signs of what was inside. Emma approached carefully, half-afraid that the rats she had sworn lived in the attic—and that Pip had named and given epic histories to when she'd told Emma and Morgan bedtime stories—would have somehow ridden down in this box and lay waiting to attack her.

But nothing so sinister awaited. Instead, the box was filled with old art supplies. Tubes and tubes of oil paints and acrylics were piled inside, along with mixing palettes and palette knives, brushes, and a few plastic cups. Emma reached down into the box, lifting two weighty handfuls of the paints, pinching one oil tube between her right index finger and thumb to find that the paint inside seemed still fluid.

She remembered her father stopping at the hardware store—Atkin's—and buying her all these the last summer he'd been alive, the summer when she and Morgan had spent nearly three months with Pip here at Cliffside. She'd been delighted that there was one little corner of the dusty mishmash of a shop that was dedicated to art supplies. She'd spent an hour selecting the brushes, running her fingers through the silky bristles, picking out all the colors of paint. It was only after her father had passed that Mr. Atkins had confessed to Emma, in low, wavering words at her father's memorial service, that her dad had pestered him every day for months to order in that art display.

Sadness filled her, but also gratitude. Her father had thought of her happiness even as his time had been running out. And here she was, fretting over whether she should cling to a relationship and a job that was wasting her time and stealing her potential for joy.

Emma remembered what she'd said to Troy last night, her final words. *I am home.*

She didn't need Los Angeles. She would stay here, at Cliffside. She would take Pip up on her offer to become the newest owner of the oldest house in town.

Decision made, heart pounding, Emma sprinted to the key holder near the kitchen sink. The keys to the truck were gone, since Pip was driving it, but a set of skeleton keys hung on the second hook, ones that Emma had always thought were decorative. But, then again, none of the doors at Cliffside had ever been locked the way they were now. The skeleton keys were her only shot aside from waiting for Pip to come home.

On her way back through the living room, Emma hefted the box of paints and swung toward the east wing of the house. As she went down the dark hall—the light switch that normally turned on the row of mosaic light fixtures mounted to the hall ceiling yielded no light at all when flicked—Emma unlocked each door she passed, delighted that the skeleton key worked. She didn't venture into any of the rooms, but some were brighter than others, and slowly the hallway filled with enough illumination that she could see down to the end, to the door that faced her at the terminus of the hallway.

The tea room door unlocked with a bit more difficulty than the other doors, the antique lock tumbling over audibly on the second try. Emma nudged into the room, holding her breath. The light switch here worked, and the tea room flooded with yellow light.

It was exactly as Emma remembered it, as though Pip had simply closed the door on the last childhood tea party that had taken place in here and forgotten all about it. The delicate floral teapot and cup set was arranged on the iron tea table, lace tablecloth draped artfully beneath. The bookshelves were still stocked with leatherbound classics that some previous generation of family had probably read, but had only been fascinating décor for a young Emma. A wingback chair faced out the large window, just waiting for someone to curl up with the knitted throw there and daydream. The wallpaper here was also peeling, and one corner of the hardwood floor was buckling, the baseboard pulling away from the wall.

But Emma knew what this place could be—could become. There had to be a way to renovate, to preserve Cliffside. It would be such a massive and overwhelming undertaking—could she handle it? She just *couldn't* let it belong to anyone else, or put it in danger of being torn down, the way she'd let her own life spiral out of her control, taking her own happiness with it.

Resolved but anxious, terrified but hopeful, Emma set the box of art supplies down on the wingback chair and reached for the curtains.

***

Pip found her a couple of hours later, just after lunch time, still in the tea room. Emma had rearranged the bookcases so that the wall that faced the window was completely bare, put away the tea set in the china cabinet in the kitchen, and even wrestled the wrought iron table out into the hallway to clear floor space. A trip to the attic had not yielded the easel that Emma hoped was still around, but Emma had improvised. A few penny nails and a stepladder later, one of the tea room's canvas curtains was tacked up on the newly blank wall, and Emma had started painting.

"Interesting," Pip said, and Emma could hear the amusement in her voice. "I love what you've done with the place."

Emma turned and smiled, then grimaced slightly and said, "I'm sorry. I hope you don't mind. I kept thinking this room was perfect for an office, but what it's really perfect for is a studio. And the curtain…"

Pip came into the room to stand beside Emma, tilting her head to look at the painting. "Pshhh. What's a few curtains when inspiration strikes?" Emma could almost feel the older woman's eyes slide over to her. "Does this mean you'll be around to hang new ones?"

Emma looked over what she'd roughed out on her makeshift canvas over the past hour, the view from the formal living room taking shape in dark streaks and light swirls. The tall grass slashed up in varying greens, and the lawn rolled away to show the sunrise just peeking up in the distance. At the edge of the lawn, Emma had added a wooden sign, a swinging placard hanging that did not yet have a name added.

"What do you think of Cliffside becoming a B and B?"

Pip grinned. "Are you kidding me? That's a fabulous thought. I used to toy with the idea, back before my arthritis got bad and all those air stay places started turning everyone's houses into vacation rentals. Too much competition."

"But none like this place," Emma said. "And now that I'm unemployed…"

"What!" Pip shrieked and clapped. "You really quit that glass zoo enclosure?"

Emma nodded, laughing. "They are emailing me like crazy. But I'm not going back. It's becoming a new habit with me, I guess."

"Good for you," Pip said. "We'll make it official tomorrow that you are the new mistress of Cliffside. Then, there's no going back. You just have to jump in."

Emma warmed inside at her aunt's encouragement. "Thank you, Pip. Really. I think this exactly what I need."

"What you need is a hammer, a good plumber, and to say some prayers. But for now," Pip said, "all the girls are here for cards. Come have lunch with us. Carol and Louise are here, and Bettie from down at the post office. I don't think you know her, but she sometimes cheats at cards, so I could use an extra set of eyes."

"You're one to talk! Bill told me how you conned him into a date."

Her aunt's side-eye was strong. "And Hallie told her mother how you practically ran over that handsome new fella who owns Curious Finds. When were you going to tell me about that?"

Emma hadn't thought of Mr. Green Eyes Great Hair since that day. And now, she was reminded of how she could never walk through downtown Haven by the Sea without a disguise on.

"Thanks, Pip. I can't have any secrets," Emma said dryly.

Laughing, Pip danced out of the tea room, beckoning Emma to follow. "Come on. The girls will have so many ideas for you."

Emma took one last glance at the drying start to her new painting, and then grabbed an old sketchbook that she had found on one of the bookshelves. She followed her aunt down the hall toward the sound of low chatter, and as she did, she reached out to run her fingers gently along the hallway wainscotting, hope fluttering in her chest.

***

The sun was setting that evening as Pip's guests left, leaving Emma with a full sketchbook and a heart brimming over with the confidence to get started. There was a new gladness in her, and Emma settled into one of the weathered rocking chairs on the wraparound porch to start organizing the project list she had started on one of the sketchbook pages. After waving goodbye to the last vehicle, Pip joined Emma on the porch, taking the chair beside her.

"Notice Bettie try to slip that ace under her salad plate?" Pip asked, lighting up a cigar that she had pulled seemingly from thin air. Emma caught the rich, vanilla-and-tobacco scent as it wafted on the cooling evening breeze.

"I did not. When?"

"Right after the third hand. It was so obvious," Pip groused.

"Ah, no. I missed it. Drat. I was talking to Louise about coming to help me clean out some of the rooms here if she's up for it. This place used to shine when she cared for it."

Pip hummed. "I bet she's happy. You know, she didn't exactly stop working for me on her own."

Emma put down her sketchbook and squinted at Pip in the waning light. "You fired her? It didn't seem like you two had any bad blood today."

"No, no." Pip drew deeply on her cigar, and the tip glowed brightly for a split second. "I started closing up the rooms and asking her back less and less. It wasn't that I couldn't afford her help, or that I didn't want her working here. It was that I couldn't help her much anymore, and it was embarrassing. All the things I used to take on myself started falling by the wayside. And I knew she could see how awful the place was getting."

Emma reached over and squeezed Pip's hand. "You should have told her. She's your friend. She would have understood."

"Yeah. And started coming over to do *more.* I just couldn't stomach having someone pity me."

"Well, it's a worry in the past," Emma reassured her. "Cliffside is going to come back, and it will be better than ever."

Emma felt a new lightness that made all the events of the past week fade away. It was about to happen—this massive house, a place she loved, was about to be renewed, reborn, and given new life, just the way Emma herself planned to be.

Now, the only problem was how to get it all done.

CHAPTER EIGHT

"What if we could just get a few rooms open by Memorial Day? Then, renting those rooms would help pay for the electrical assessment for the main panel in the basement. Then, we could aim to be fully operational by summer."

Emma looked up from her laptop at Louise, feeling the stress of the week starting to overwhelm her. Louise was calmly taking cushion and pillow covers off all the couches and chairs that had been crowded into the formal living room, examining each to see if any of them needed repair.

What a difference a week made.

Since deciding to accept Pip's transfer of ownership to Cliffside, Emma felt she had not been still for more than the scant hours of sleep that she'd been getting. It was a good tired, an accomplished tired, but Emma was bone-deep exhausted all the same. All the papers were now signed, and Emma was officially responsible for the house.

There was a landscaping company to arrange for the jungle of grass and rose bushes and hedges that had become the front lawn; an arborist to selectively trim the towering trees that sheltered the house itself. Then, a "driveway guy" who drove from Carmel, walking up and down the rutted and crumbling gravel driveway that led to the main road, clipboard in hand, presenting Emma with a list of asphalt choices and top seal options and a line-by-line list, one line of which was the project cost of grading machinery. That number had almost made her faint.

And Emma hadn't even begun to tackle the inside of the house. Oh, she'd opened all the rooms now, and she'd helped Pip select the furniture that had been subsequently moved from Cliffside to the new house, but the buckled floors and stuck windows and ominous pipe noises preyed on Emma's every waking hour.

Then, there was the trouble with LA—arranging a real estate agent to get the Los Angeles house on the market, movers to pack up her things and send them to Cliffside, and making sure through her shiny, new divorce attorney that the process of untangling herself from Troy would be as fast as possible. The divorce papers were due to be served to Troy in the near future. She'd almost asked to have him served at the gym, or at Trish's house out of spite—though she had no idea if her ex-best-friend and soon-to-be-ex-husband were even speaking anymore.

Emma wished that Pip were here still, but she'd taken over Cliffside so that her aunt could get some rest and relief from the stress of the house. She'd tried hard not to call Pip at every little issue that had popped up over the past week. Pip should enjoy the new place without worrying over Emma.

"Three or four rooms?" Louise questioned, yanking a striped cover off the seat of a divan, coughing at the dust that rose in the morning light. "Including your room? Or would you have the guests in the other wing?"

Emma considered. Having guests in the same wing as her room would mean less privacy, but putting them in the *other* wing would mean she would need to fix the electrical problem that had caused the hallway and several bedrooms over there to have no power.

"I don't know, *petit chou,*" Louise said. "That's still a lot of work, and so little time."

Emma smiled at the nickname the Frenchwoman had used for any child in her circle since Emma could recall. "I'm neither little, nor a cabbage. I do have a little *amount* of cabbage, however…"

Sighing, Emma brought up her bank account, a nice, fresh one that was hers and hers alone—another step toward untangling from Troy. The balance was less than fresh, however.

"It'll have to be the wing I'm in for now. At least we paid the contractor to get started there already."

"You picked which one?" Louise asked. "Not the guy who said he would just spackle over that crack in the wall in the green bathroom?"

"He was the cheapest, but no. And not the guy who had the weird van and wanted to live on-property while he 'oversaw construction and security.' So creepy."

"So who?" Louise sorted a cushion cover into the "mend" pile.

"Remember the fella who was by on Tuesday? The one who didn't tell me to tear the house down and start over. Kind of looks like a country music singer, had the boots and the cowboy hat? His quote was reasonable, he was fine to let us take care of cosmetic stuff like painting, and he was very knowledgeable about the underlying structure of the house. He said he'll start on Monday."

Emma sat staring at the bank balance, still fretting. She was saved momentarily by the sound of the doorbell echoing through the house. She closed her laptop and waited. The doorbell came again.

"Expecting someone?" Louise asked.

Emma shook her head, unfolding from her place on one of the cushion-bare couches to trot to the massive front door. She swung it open to reveal a woman standing there—but she was no one that Emma recognized.

"Can I help you?" she asked the tall redhead, who would have reminded her of Hallie Nelson, if she hadn't had six inches on Emma's old friend, or a head of wild curls instead of Hallie's long, straight hair.

"I can help *you*," the woman said assertively. She looked about Emma's age, and she was wearing dark jeans, a worn baseball tee, and a tool belt that was fully loaded with hand tools. "Lola Quinn, the Handy Madame. I heard that Cliffside had a new owner, and I've been dying to get a look inside for years. You her?"

Emma swung open the screen door and stepped out onto the porch. "That's me. Emma Sullivan." She offered a hand, and Lola shook it, already wandering down the porch and looking up at the gingerbread that edged the eaves.

"Lots of this can be preserved. And what needs to be replaced can be replicated—cut at the sawmill. No need to go the fancy places that sell vintage trim. Plus, you get the benefit of local wood that is already acclimated to the environment."

As Emma watched, Lola whipped out a measuring tape and squatted, assessing the length between the porch floor and where the front steps touched the uneven ground.

"I just hired a contractor. I'm so sorry you came all the way up here. I mean if you came from the cove…"

"Yep. Been here two years. Ask around. I do good work, anytime anyone gives me a chance. Got my own tools, got my own truck to haul supplies." Lola threw a thumb toward a pickup truck that Emma could see parked just beyond the tall grass. The truck was painted an army green, but Emma could see that big, plastic eyelashes had been added to the front headlights. In bright pink letters across the side of the truck scrolled the words "The Handy Madame – Get the Gal Who Nails It Every Time!"

Lola continued. ""I might not have a big crew, but I'm a hard worker. And you might already have someone in mind, but let me leave my card. In case you change your mind." Lola still wasn't looking at

Emma, but at the railing of the porch, tracing her fingers over the twists of the rail supports with something like reverence. With her other hand, Lola untucked a business card—complete with her name, number, and a cartoon rendering of the green pickup—and handed it over to Emma.

There was something so sweet and earnest about this woman, scoping out Emma's front porch as though she were viewing an art exhibit at the Louvre, that hit Emma in the heart. Surely, Lola couldn't handle all the repairs and arrangements that Cliffside would need. Emma couldn't hire her over the cowboy foreman with the six-man crew.

But it was obvious that Lola was fascinated by the house. And maybe Emma could find a project or two that she might help with. Just small things. To give the woman a chance.

Emma looked at the card for a moment, and then back at Lola. "You want to come inside for some coffee and a look around?" she offered.

Lola smiled wide, meeting Emma's eyes for only the second time since she'd arrived. Her blue eyes were lit and the excitement evident in her voice. "Could I? That would be *great*!"

Emma stepped back into the house, smiling, and held open the screen door for the other woman to enter.

CHAPTER NINE

When Emma heard the front door open, she and Lola had just been sitting down in the kitchen for some fresh coffee. Louise had taken a cup to go and waved goodbye airily with promises to return with the mended cushion covers tomorrow. Perhaps too wary from her years in Los Angeles, Emma had stiffened at the sound, grabbing a spatula that sat on a nearby counter as the sound of the door shutting echoed from the front hall and back toward the kitchen. Lola—completely unbidden—had abandoned her stool at the kitchen island and hustled to the stove, where the old-fashioned stainless percolator sat, still warm.

Between them, Emma was sure they'd made a truly terrifying duo—ready to spatula and scald whoever was walking down the hall. It hadn't been long before the sound of the *several* people (of varying statures) who had invaded floated down the passageway. The chatter had been as recognizable to Emma as the sound of her own voice, and she'd instantly relaxed.

She'd put out a hand to Lola, inwardly impressed at her new friend's fierceness in the face of potential danger.

"At ease, girl. It's just my sister."

And moments later, Morgan appeared in the kitchen doorway, with Tilly and Daniel in tow. She was carrying several plastic grocery bags, and as she marched toward the island, Emma could see that Daniel carried a small crate full of paintbrushes, and Tilly was wheeling a wagon filled with a couple dozen paint sample cans.

Morgan, seeing Lola with the coffee pot still at the ready, stopped short. "Oh! Hi, Ems. Hi…person who looks like she's about to scald me with a coffee pot."

Emma had a new house, was meeting lots of new friends, reuniting with old ones, and getting a fresh new start—and on top of that, she'd almost just assaulted her own sister in the kitchen. Her day was just getting more and more exciting.

Emma put her attack spatula on the island and moved to help Morgan with two of the bags. "This is Lola. She's here to tour the house and figure out what she can help with on the renovation. Lola, this is Morgan, and my niece and nephew, Tilly and Daniel."

Lola waved and surreptitiously slid the coffee pot back onto the stovetop.

As Emma put the crate on the island, Morgan said brightly, "Great! That must be your truck out front. That's what we came for. What's a nice Saturday for if it can't be for helping here?"

A crash sounded behind Morgan, and Emma turned from the island to see paintbrushes scattering across the kitchen floor. Daniel stood shellshocked, staring wide-eyed at the crate, which now had a broken handle on one side. "Oops. I did not mean for *that* to happen," he said.

Tilly burst into laughter, but made no move to help her brother. Daniel turned bright red in the face and swiveled to glare at her.

"That's okay," Lola said, moving to help him as he ended his death stare and knelt to pick the brushes up. "I'll help you."

Emma smiled at the pair and walked to Tilly, giving her a pointed look, a side hug, and taking the wagon handle from her hand. "Be nice to your brother," she whispered, and then, louder, "What's all this, Morgan?"

Emma pulled the wagon over the threshold from the hall to the kitchen as Morgan emptied the other two bags she'd carried onto the island. Emma saw paint stirrers, wide, flat spackle knives, and a few catalogs. "This is me trying to apply the random knowledge that I retained from being an interior design school dropout. I have brought fabric samples for curtains"—she pointed to the catalogs—"and paint samples for the walls, and a few small containers of different textures of plaster so we can see what you like best to repair the ceilings."

Lola seemed to perk at the mention of the plaster. She stood from the floor, all the paintbrushes now back in the crate, and came to the island, peering inside the still-packed other bags. "You have different kinds of plaster with you?"

"Yup."

"I like you already," Lola said, chuckling.

"Morgan, thank you." Emma took the crate of paintbrushes from Daniel and placed it on one of the stools at the island. "But you guys don't have to help me. I wasn't planning to actually start any projects myself, today."

"Nonsense," Morgan replied, holding her hands out so that Daniel and Tilly would come over. When they did, she grasped their hands in hers and lifted all their arms together. "We are Team Cliffside! We will be here every weekend until this place shines like the top of the Chrysler Building. And *you* have to pick out paint colors and fabric and plaster just to start. There will be many more decisions to make in the future. Exterior paint, wainscotting and chair rails, or smooth walls? What about the built-in bookcases in the library? Keeping those or ripping them out to make another bedroom? I mean, that's one more room to rent, but the loss of that rolling ladder would be a *crime*."

Emma blinked. "The library stays. I'm not a criminal. Everything else—yikes. What do we have to do *today*?"

"Good. I'll walk you through everything." Morgan dropped Tilly and Daniel's hands. "Now, kids. Upstairs in the attic there is a roll of plastic sheeting. Can you go up—together—and bring it down? It should be right inside the hatch. We used it to pack up some of Aunt Pip's stuff for the move."

Tilly and Daniel both grinned and nodded, and then took off back down the hall jostling and bickering lightly over who got to go up the ladder first.

"They are just tornados made of sass and opposition today," Morgan said. She sighed heavily, and then pointed at Emma. "You're going to want to grab something to write with. Our first step is a house tour."

Lola let out a quiet, "Yes!" beside Emma, and Emma scanned the kitchen for her planning sketchpad.

Scooping it up from where it sat on one of the other island barstools, she brandished it at Morgan. "Already got something." In fact, Emma thought she might have to get a new sketchpad soon. Her ideas for Cliffside were practically overflowing in this one.

Above their heads, Emma could hear Tilly and Daniel bring the attic ladder down—with a hard *thunk*—onto the floor. Then, more bickering—louder this time—and the sound of something heavy rolling down steps, coming to rest with an even louder crash. She winced when a small cloud of dust showered down from the crumbling ceiling over the eat-in space of the kitchen. Could Cliffside stand up to her niece and nephew?

"Everyone okay up there?" Morgan called, and Tilly and Daniela answered in uncertain unison.

After a moment, the kids came back downstairs, lugging a fairly bulky roll of plastic sheeting between them. Daniel's hair stuck out at all angles, and Tilly was coated in dust. They dropped the plastic sheeting on the kitchen floor, and Daniel reached up to knock dust bunnies from his own hair.

"I fell down the attic stairs," Tilly said matter-of-factly. "I think I have internal injuries."

"Oh, you do?" Morgan said, looking amused.

"You can't see them because they are *in*ternal. And the hospital in Haven is too small to have the right diagnostics."

Lola guffawed. "How in the world do you know the word *diagnostics*?"

"She watches a lot of medical dramas," Morgan explained, beginning to rummage through the paint samples in the wagon. She motioned Emma to her and began handing tiny paint cans over, which Emma gathered in a bent arm.

"You'll have to take me somewhere with better standard of care," Tilly explained, kicking at the corner of a warped floorboard. "Somewhere like…"

"*Tilly Marie Taylor*, if you say Los Angeles one more time, I will ship you there in a Fed-Ex box. Aunt Emma is here in Cliffside indefinitely. So stop. Now, come over here and carry some paint samples."

This time, it was Daniel who laughed and pointed as Tilly sulked over. "Tilly wants to go to Hollywood because she thinks she can be a movie star!"

Tilly stuck her tongue out at Daniel and made a face. "At least that's more interesting than thinking you can play video games for a job when you grow up," she countered.

"Both of you," Morgan said, "will fit in one big Fed-Ex box. And then, you can work out your problems on the way to mutual big-screen and virtual success." She passed three samples to Tilly, who fell into agitated silence. Emma tried valiantly to hold back her own laughter.

Lola tilted her head toward the hallway. "You mind if I take your fella so he can help me get some tools from the truck?"

Morgan shrugged. "Not at all."

At Emma's questioning look, Lola said, "I figure the best way to apply for the job of helping with this place is to just spend a day helping. What do you say?"

Paint samples, plaster samples, recreating the outside trim…

The library, the curtains, and what will you do with that one broken pane from the stained glass in the back stairwell?

Emma was feeling overwhelmed again. But standing in front of her was Lola, willing to help. Morgan, willing to help. And Tilly and Daniel—willing to help as long as it got them out of their house chores and let them explore Cliffside's many fascinating nooks and crannies, she would bet.

"I think that would be great," she said, letting her shoulders relax. "Get what you need, and you and Daniel meet us in the library upstairs. Come up the stairs, turn right down the hall, and it'll be the third door on your left."

Lola saluted and turned to Daniel. "Okay, sir. How do you feel about wearing a tool belt?"

Daniel's eyes widened. "Like, I get to carry my own tools?"

She nodded. "I told your aunt here that I have a small crew. It was true, of course. It's the smallest you can get and not have zero—it's just me. But if you're up for it, I'd love to add you to my employee roster. That will make us a crew of two. What do you say?"

His eyes darted to Morgan, and Emma saw the glint of interest in his gaze. There was nothing that Daniel liked more than feeling as though he were getting to do something grown-up.

"Your choice," Morgan said, playing deftly into Daniel's personality.

"What's the pay?" Daniel asked, planting his hands on his hips.

"Well," Lola said. "There will be a two-weekend probationary period where I assess your work. That's like a *diagnosis*, see?" She looked pointedly over at Tilly and grinned, and Tilly grinned back.

"But then, if I decide you're doing pretty good and working hard—even if you don't know something, but you're trying and learning and getting better—I could give you ten dollars a week."

Emma leaned against the island, watching Daniel do a calculation in his head. "That means if I work for one month and do good, I could buy *GrandRace 7.0* and not have to wait for my birthday!"

Lola nodded. "Whatever that is, bud. Sure."

Daniel leapt into the air, fist-pumped, and zoomed down the hall. Emma heard him fling open the front door, a feat for his age and the weight of the thing.

"He's probably already climbing in your truck for a hammer," Morgan said, laughter shaking her shoulders. "How come he doesn't do that when I ask him to clean his room? He gets allowance!"

"Novelty," Lola said. "What is he, eight?"

"Seven." Morgan peered down the hall.

"My son is eight," Lola said. "And no amount of money I could offer him would make him help me on a job. The kid is stuck in his computer programming. Builds robots and all. I guess they just like what's new. It'll wear off, so we'd better take advantage of the extra help now."

"I can help too!" Tilly said, reminding the three women that she was still there.

"Yes, you can," Morgan said, nodding toward the front living room. "And I will gladly match Miss Lola's salary for Daniel for you if you will be my assistant interior designer. Deal? Maybe one day, you'll look back on this and say that this is where your flashy designer-to-the-stars career started. Just don't forget me when you're picking out couches for the rich and famous in *Los Angeles*."

Tilly pursed her lips. "Mom. You said no more talk about—"

"Okay, okay. You're right. C'mon."

Emma watched as Lola took off to the front yard to equip Daniel with his tool belt and tools, and Morgan and Tilly made their way into the front living room, chatting about the colors they carried and which samples should be swiped on which walls.

Standing in the kitchen, which seemed to be becoming the center of most of the recent activity at Cliffside, Emma smiled at how her unplanned day had suddenly turned busy—in the best way. Things felt so different here. Despite the fact that her living arrangements hadn't changed all that much—she was still alone at Cliffside the same way she'd been the majority of the time at her own home in LA—being here felt warm, and welcoming, and like the silence that fell at night was full of promise and new things to come instead of just cold loneliness. It was a stark contrast to the way she'd felt just weeks ago, even with her high-powered job and years of accomplishment. Why had it taken coming to a crumbling house to make her realize that her life had been crumbling beforehand?

Morgan's head popped back into the kitchen. "Ems? You coming?"

Emma startled and nodded. "Yes! Yes, I'm coming."

She bustled toward the living room, tightening her arms around the half-dozen paint sample cans she carried. It was time to get to work.

CHAPTER TEN

It was the mold that finally got them. But it was also the mold that redirected Emma to something wonderful—one of Cliffside's many secrets that just might turn out to be the solution to one of Emma's problems.

Four hours into their work, while in the library sorting out which furniture to keep and which to get rid of, Emma came upon a divan that had a whole forest of mold growing on it. It hadn't been visible at first, but she flipped up a cushion to see that the cream-colored fabric was completely covered in bright green on the underside, and the musty smell that wafted up immediately made her eyes water.

"Ewwww, gross!" Tilly shrieked, immediately abandoning her assistant interior designer duties for the less-smelly location of the hallway. Then, when the smell hit her even out there, she pinched her nose closed and said in a nasally voice, "Moooom, can I go down to the kitchen and get a snack?"

"Definitely gross," Morgan agreed, peering over Emma's shoulder. "And maybe not so safe. We should open the windows and clear out the air in here."

Emma looked over at Tilly. "There are cookies in the blue jar on the counter, and there's milk in the fridge."

After a nod from Morgan, Tilly whooshed downstairs. Setting the cushion down gingerly to avoid a shower of goodness knows what kind of spores, Emma beat a hasty retreat for the big, floor to ceiling windows on one side of the library, while Morgan went for the other side. They got five of the six windows open, and only the sixth—to the left of the big, stone fireplace—was stuck closed. As the salty spring air whooshed in, dissipating the stagnant smell of the moldy settee, Emma leaned on the windowsill that had opened on the opposite side of the mantel, looking out over the side yard of Cliffside.

Daniel and Lola were on the roof of the gazebo that sat in the side garden, and from her vantage point, Emma could see Lola showing Daniel how to line up a hammer on the head of a nail, tapping lightly to set the point before striking hard to bury the fastener into the new shingles they were placing. After a couple demonstrations, Daniel tried it—and was successful. Emma beamed at his triumphant expression, looking back over her shoulder at Morgan, who was slowly pulling sheets off the other furniture in the library.

"Danny's doing great! I'm surprised you got him out of the house and over here."

Morgan laughed. "Yes, well, now that Lola has promised him a 401k and stock options, you won't be able to get rid of him." She came to join Emma at the window, and they both watched as Daniel and Lola made quick work of a whole row of new shingles. "I like her. What's her story?"

Emma shrugged. "I don't know. I figured you knew her—or, at least, of her. She says she's been here two years."

"And her son is eight. I bet Danny knows more about him than I would about Lola. But I haven't seen her at any of the school events or at church or anything. I mean, I've seen her truck around town. It's hard to miss." Morgan pushed away from the window and resumed uncovering the furniture, tensing as though a bomb might go off as she pulled another sheet.

"Is it ever! Those lashes belong on camera."

Morgan twisted up the sheet she'd just tugged free. "If you say anything about Los Angeles, I will stuff you in that box with my children."

Emma moved from the window to test the library ladder, and when she found it sturdy, climbed up a few rungs and began taking down books. "You wouldn't. Once I'm gone, Pip will make you take this place. And you see now how much work it's going to be." She set a few disintegrating books on the mantel, reshelving two that were still worth keeping.

As they both lapsed into comfortable silence, working, Emma thought about Lola—what was her story? She seemed happy, upbeat, and she was funny and personable. Why hadn't her involved-in-everything sister ever met the handywoman before? Another mystery, one to add to the questions about Emma's parents. Cliffside felt more classic and Gothic than ever. Emma hoped they wouldn't find any long-lost relatives in a secret room somewhere.

Her morbid train of thought was derailed when she pulled a book free of the shelf and it made a distinct, metallic *rattle*. It startled her so much that she reared away from the shelving, and only by pure luck regained her composure enough to grasp the ladder before she fell backward off it. The book tumbled out of her hand, bounced off the bottom rung of the library ladder, and landed on the fraying carpet. As it settled, it cracked open—and a glittering, tangled pile of jewelry cascaded out.

Morgan had turned when Emma had started to fall, and she met Emma's eyes with a wide-eyed stare of her own. On the carpet were necklaces, bracelets, and what looked to be several pairs of elaborate earrings.

"Holy moly," Morgan said. "Treasure."

Emma turned back to the bookshelf. The book she'd pulled off, the one that had just turned out to be hollow and full of hidden jewels, had been the first of a set. The rest of the series—*The History of the Forgotten World, Volumes Two through Four*—was still sitting unassumingly on the shelf, under a half inch of dust.

Emma pulled book two and flipped open the cover. Inside, it was also hollow, housing rings and a gold-tone belt that was studded with what appeared to be emeralds. Emma's ears began to feel hot.

"Pass them down! Pass them down!" Morgan said, reaching up and making grabby hands. Emma passed down the second volume and reached for the other two.

Books three and four were similarly full of goodies, and Emma climbed down after fetching them, kneeling to the carpet to pick up one of the fallen necklaces. "What do you think these are? *Whose* do you think these are?"

"I don't know," Morgan said, sifting through the pile of rings in book two. "We should ask Pip. She would know." She held up a particularly ornate ring, gasping at it. "Ems, some of these look valuable. This could be the answer to your budget problem. Find out what these babies are worth, and put that money toward some new furniture. Y'know, some that isn't growing mushrooms."

Emma had gathered most of the fallen jewelry and returned it to the first book, and now she stacked them all together, taking the book out of Morgan's hands to place it in the proper order with the rest. "I don't know. The money would be Pip's, not mine. And no way would I buy new furniture. Maybe just new to me. But still old. I want Cliffside to look like, well, Cliffside. A moment in time, but not *ravaged* by it. "

"Let's call her," Morgan suggested. "We could all use some lunch, and I think a break is in order. Leave these windows open, and we'll see what those paint swatches we painted on the far wall look like in afternoon light when we get back. Pip can come to town with us and eat. There's a new antiques shop just up the street from Sunnyside

Diner. We could go check it out for furniture. And maybe the owner might know something about all this jewelry."

Emma felt her face flush at the mention of the antiques shop. *That* shop. The one owned by the ruggedly handsome victim of her first social *faux pas* after arriving in town.

"I'm not sure…"

"Sure, you are. It's been ages since you had the Baja tacos at Sunnyside. C'mon." Morgan jostled her lightly with a shoulder.

Emma looked at the stack of hollowed-out books. She was a little nervous to go into town, having been avoiding it and the memories that might lurk there. But she didn't need to be stuck in the past. In fact, what she needed to do was solve a mystery—the mystery of this trove of jewelry that had fallen on them, literally. And if she had to grin and bear it in front of the guy she'd made into a latte waterfall, well, new Emma could do it. She didn't shrink from confrontation anymore. And she had no excuse not to go into town anymore, ever since she'd had her car brought from Los Angeles to Haven. The shiny SUV sat in the gravel drive, just waiting to be taken through the picture-perfect streets of downtown. And Emma could fit Morgan and both kids in there.

"Ok, yes," she said, picking up two of the books. Morgan followed suit, and Emma strode toward the library door. "And I'm getting the Baja tacos *and* a coconut-lime slushy. Extra whip."

"You rebel," Morgan said as she followed her out. Then, after a beat, she said, "If these things make us rich, promise me you'll help me keep Tilly from whining to move to LA."

***

Main street was bustling as Emma, Morgan, Tilly, Daniel, and Lola made their way down the sidewalk to the Sunnyside Diner. Lola had come after a lot of cajoling from Daniel, who was now plying her with questions about her son. Emma tried her best to listen to Morgan talk and keep an ear on Daniel so he didn't bombard Lola too much. The work she'd done at Cliffside today had convinced Emma to hire Lola as a go-to set of extra hands. She didn't want the woman to run screaming into the woods because of Danny's boyish overwhelmingness.

As Morgan pointed out things that had changed along the small strip of shops downtown, and Emma waved at a few passers-by who called out in recognition, Emma heard—

"But why doesn't he go to school? I mean, like, *real* school? And does that mean he doesn't have weekends off school? Where is he right now?"

Lola's laugh was light, but Emma looked back to see that the woman's face bore an odd expression. "He is with his grandma right now in Carmel, visiting. You know, where Pip's new house is? The same city. And, well, when we moved here, he had a bit of trouble fitting in. So we found him a school program on the computer that he follows. So he does go to *real school*, just not the way you do. He has teachers, classmates, and clubs. Remember I said he builds robots? They do that at the library every Monday night. It's a STEM club. Next month, they're building their own video games. You should check it out."

"Okay. That could be cool." Emma could see the barely contained excitement in Daniel's eyes. "Would your son—what's his name?"

"His name is Ethan," Lola said.

"Would Ethan want me to go?"

"I'm sure as soon as he meets you, he'll be glad you came. He'll love that you're so into games."

"Awesome." Daniel's grin lasted all the way to the diner, and as they all filed in, Emma dropped back to talk to Lola. The big canvas bag that she carried, which contained all the hollowed-out books filled with jewelry, bumped against her leg as she stopped.

"Thanks for your help today," she said, putting a hand out so that Lola would hang back outside the diner door. "And for getting Daniel excited about working. It can be hard on Morgan with four of them, and Danny's in the middle, so he gets lost sometimes. I think he really liked being out one-on-one with you today."

"I get it. I wish Ethan was so excited to hang out with me. Only child. One parent. We can get on each other's nerves." Lola laughed, which seemed to come easy, but there was a flash of sadness that pricked Emma's heart. She didn't want to pry, but she sensed that maybe Lola had some heartbreak in her past, maybe just like Emma was going through now.

"No kids for me yet, but I'm sure at some point in life, I will be begging you for advice. You seem like an awesome mom."

Lola blinked. "Oh. Thanks." And then, the redhead blushed lightly. "You guys are being so kind. I mean, I haven't really made friends since we moved here. It's nice to finally get to hang out with people who aren't waiting on a quote for new drywall."

Emma peered through the front windows of Sunnyside. She could see that Morgan and the kids had found Pip, and Pip was directing another table to be scooted up to theirs to fit their group size. Daniel and Tilly were drifting toward the open doorway to the arcade that was adjacent to the diner. Emma remembered many a Friday night spent first at dinner at Sunnyside, followed by a mad dash through the door that connected the diner to the arcade, the noise and lights just too much to resist.

"About that," Emma said, turning back to Lola, "how would you like to join *my* small crew?"

"You mean come work on Cliffside? I would love it!" Lola's face lit up like a tree on Christmas.

"Nothing big, you know. I do have a contractor coming to do some foundation repair and roofing and to tear down that awful storage shed at the back of the property. But I could use help inside, with the paint and the baseboards and"—Emma groaned—"maybe the floors?"

"The floors will be a feat," Lola agreed.

"So you're in?" Emma could see Pip waving them inside.

"I'm in," Lola said, smiling brightly.

Everything was falling into place. Emma couldn't have felt more buoyant as she opened the door to Sunnyside, and she and Lola slipped inside. Daniel introduced Lola to Pip, Pip immediately asked Lola if she could drive the eyelash pickup truck, and they all settled into their seats to peruse the menu. They managed to all order—with Emma insisting on coconut-lime slushies for the whole table—and update Pip on all the work that had been done at Cliffside completely before the subject of the jewelry came up.

"Well, let's see it," Pip said, moving the water glasses and silverware around her to make a wide, cleared spot on the table.

Emma handed over the first book, and everyone at the table seemed to hold their collective breath. Pip sifted through the necklaces, set out the pairs of earrings, and finally picked up one of the chunkier silver bracelets of the lot.

"None of this looks familiar," she admitted after a length of study. "I honestly have no idea who this belonged to. My mother never wore jewelry, and I don't know if I ever saw my grandmother wear much more than her wedding ring and a set of pearls that my grandfather gave her. This looks older than even those generations, though."

Morgan lifted her slushy glass and slurped through the straw, cutting her eyes over at Emma. "I told her to take them all to Timeless Treasures. She could ask the new guy what they're worth."

Pip's eyes lit up—brighter than Lola's had earlier if it were possible.

Don't say it, Pip, Emma thought. *Don't say it.*

"Emma! You should. You could make it up to him for practically drowning the poor, attractive dear in coffee. Take him the jewelry, see what he says, and ask him out."

"Eww, gross," Tilly said, wrinkling her nose. Another phrase for Tilly bingo. Apparently, mold *and* boys were gross. Emma made a mental note to let her know that Los Angeles was full of both of those things—a fact that she was sure Morgan would be grateful to her for imparting. Score one for Aunt Emma.

Morgan dug in her purse and came up with some stray cash, which she handed to Tilly and Daniel. "Why don't you two go play in the arcade?"

The siblings didn't argue about that.

When the kids were out of earshot, Emma leaned over her slushie and said, "Pip, I'm not on the market."

"You mean legally? Well, living well is the best revenge, I say. You're young, pretty, and he didn't go to high school with you. I mean, the options for eligible, tolerable-looking men are pretty slim in Haven."

"Amen, sister," Lola said, reaching across the table to high-five Pip.

"Great, now you're all forming a gang," Emma groused. "I'm just not interested in dating. I'm…emotionally fragile."

"Pffft," Morgan joined in. "Scared, you mean. Do you guys want dessert?"

Emma started to protest Morgan's words—but not dessert, since Sunnyside had the world's best fried ice cream—but Lola jumped in.

"So what if Emma is scared? I mean, I don't know anything about your love life"—Lola stirred her own slushie, staring down into the glass—"but I do know what it's like to be nervous to get back out there. I went on a few dates when we first arrived, but, man, it just isn't the same as when I was dating back in my twenties. It used to be that all I wanted was a handsome face, a good time, and not to have to pay for my own dinner. Now, I have so many danged requirements, I'd be surprised if any guy in or out of Haven could fit them all."

Pip nodded sagely. "You live, you love, and you form a long list of preferences."

The waiter appeared, and Pip ordered four fried ice cream bowls for the table, asking for two more with cones packed to go for Tilly and Daniel. Scribbling their order down, he disappeared into the back kitchen.

"Is that the problem?" Morgan snickered as she looked directly at Emma. "You have too many standards?"

"No," Emma said vehemently. Then, after a pause to think, she added, "Well, there are a few things I would change if I had to pick someone new. Different from Troy."

"Her ex," Morgan whispered to Lola, who nodded.

"Not a cheater," Pip offered.

"Definitely not," Emma agreed. "And the new guy would chew with his mouth closed. And not use any internet slang in regular conversation."

"LOL," Morgan said, and Emma pitched a crumpled-up napkin at her, which she dodged.

"And actually have a job—I mean, something where he needs a skill that involves thought—*not* just some lip-service management position at a fancy 'wellness compendium.'"

"It was a gym with a juice bar," Morgan snorted. "And his daddy got him a franchise of it."

"And the new guy would never feel threatened by my drive or intelligence. And he would open doors for me. Heck, he would even wait until I got out of a cab before he started walking to the door. I mean, this one time, it was pouring rain when we went to one of my client's work events in LA, and Troy—" Something caught in Emma's throat before she could get the rest of the story out, and she suddenly found herself choking back a sob.

The sob became two, and then tears spilled over her lashes.

"Oh, honey," Pip said, and Morgan and Lola both made fretting noises as all three women moved into a huddle around Emma. Pip grabbed a hand, Lola grabbed a hand, and Morgan, who was sitting beside her, hugged Emma close.

"S-s-sorry," she said, mortified. "I don't know why…"

"Yes, you do," Morgan said gently. "For the same reason that you know why you're here, back home. You need to be and stay as far away from Troy as possible. That man was and is *absolutely* awful. He treated you like dirt. And not even expensive, organic gardening soil.

Like shoe dirt. The dirt that gets into your shoe by accident, and you have to stop and get it out because it's so annoying when it gets between your sock and insole."

Emma nodded, laughing through her tears, her chest burning with the pain of emotions that she was choking back. "I know. I know."

It was then that they looked up to see the waiter standing nearby with a tray loaded down with their ice cream bowls. He was staring at them, obviously uncomfortable.

"Uh, everything okay?" he asked, shuffling forward a step.

"Yes, excellent," Pip replied, not missing a beat. "But can we get our check now? My niece really needs to go flirt with the guy who owns Timeless Treasures."

CHAPTER ELEVEN

Emma practiced a few flirty lines in her head as she walked briskly up Main Street toward the bank, the same direction that Timeless Treasures was in. When everything she rehearsed sounded cheesy and overdone, she decided that she would just stick with an apology and ask for advice. Behind her, trailing after like some sort of small-town parade, were her sister, Tilly and Daniel, Pip, and Lola, all as conspicuous as if it had actually been the Fourth of July, and they'd all been carrying lit sparklers.

As they neared the bright red awning with the Timeless Treasures sign swinging beneath it, Emma stopped and turned to the line of people behind her.

"I think you should all go. Don't follow me in."

"Why?" Morgan asked, crossing her arms over her chest. "I thought we were going to look at furniture together."

"I am going in to ask him about the jewels—"

"And flirt a little," Pip reminded her.

"Nope. Give it a rest!" Emma shook the canvas bag that contained the hollowed books. "Just the jewels. And if I spot anything good in there, Morgan, then I will text you. But you should all scatter. Go."

There were a smattering of protests, but Lola put her fingers between her lips and whistled piercingly, quieting the group. "Hey! Why don't we all head down to the hardware store and get what we need to fix that stuck window in the library? And Daniel and me could use another box of nails for the gazebo roof."

Reluctantly, the group agreed, and Lola turned on her heel and marched ahead, leading the group in the opposite direction down the sidewalk.

Emma liked her more and more.

After she'd waited a good five minutes as the merry band had disappeared around a corner on their way to Atkin's Hardware, Emma steeled herself, walked to the heavy glass door of Timeless Treasures, and yanked it open before she could change her mind. A soft multi-note chime sounded from a bell mounted above the door, but there was no one in sight as she stepped into the store.

Emma took the chance to browse on her own, wondering at the number of items that were packed into what she had thought was a small space. But the main room opened into two side rooms, and there wasn't a square inch of the place that was ill-used. Couches, chairs, and dinettes were set up at various places, and other pieces were arranged around them as if one had walked into a room of a house. Delicate vintage dish sets sat ready for a dinner party on heavy wooden tabletops, and wingbacks and curved divans clustered around marble coffee and accent tables that had ornately carved legs. Retro advertising signs hung over bookshelves lined with leather volumes and ephemera. The entire place smelled like a library and secret attic in a storybook—dust and leather and lost stories layered with the wafting, ozone scent of slight dampness and warmed wax. Emma circled through one of the side rooms and back up to the still-empty front, where a vanilla candle burned on the checkout counter.

Someone must be here. Surely, the owner wouldn't have left a lit candle in a shop full of old paper and wood unattended.

"Hello?" She hated how uncertain she sounded. No way did she sound like that presenting to a client, marking out roles for her staff in a new campaign, or drawing up a multi-million-dollar ad budget for a company. So why did she sound that way now?

Emma squared her shoulders, marched to the front counter, and hit the small service bell that sat there several times.

"Hello!" she called more assertively.

There was a heavy red velvet curtain over a doorway behind the counter, and it moved, and then was brushed aside as Mr. Windswept and Smouldery came out from whatever was back there.

"Oh, hey!" he said, seeming to recognize her instantly. Emma shrank inside, but managed to maintain her confident posture as he stepped around the counter and walked to her side. "You're the new owner of Cliffside. Is it—Emma, yes?"

He hadn't said *That girl who doused me in hot coffee*, so maybe that hadn't made as big an impression as Emma had thought. Her nerves lessened a little.

"That's me," she said, taking the hand he offered and shaking it. "Emma Sullivan. Yes, of Cliffside." *Of Cliffside? What is this, a Regency novel?* She kept her smile plastered on. "Nice to meet you—it was Hudson, right?"

His hand was broad, and warm, and there was a slight roughness to his palm that said he wasn't just a shopkeeper. He worked with his hands—in some capacity. Emma tried not to swoon toward him when she noticed the laugh lines that crinkled at the corners of his eyes when he smiled at her.

"Hudson Ford, of the Endless Harbor Fords, which means nothing to you because this is California and not the East Coast. But trust me, we're very upper middle-class. You would know us if you were in a specific area of Maine that spans a few dozen miles."

"Charmed, I'm sure," she replied. He was still holding onto her hand, even though they'd finished shaking. He had really nice arms, she imagined, judging by the pleasing shape of them under the sleeves of his long-sleeved gray T-shirt.

He squinted at her, took a deep breath, and pulled his hand gently from her grip. "Can I, uh, help you find something?"

Remembering why she was here—which was definitely *not* to imagine Hudson Ford woodworking in a fitted flannel shirt with the sleeves rolled up—Emma hoisted the canvas bag into view. "Actually, no. I already find—*found*—something at the house that I wanted your professional opinion on."

A glint of interest flashed in his eyes. "Intriguing. Let's see what you've got." Instead of moving to the counter when he gestured to it, Emma stood there, staring at his crinkly crow's feet.

Dang. Fail.

He tapped the counter lightly, and she managed to be almost completely unawkward as she moved to the empty spot next to the antique register and began to unload the hollowed-out books. She lined them all up side by side, and then flipped each open to reveal the contents.

"We found these in the Cliffside library. No one knows anything about them. Would you mind taking a look? I can pay you if you can appraise them…"

Hudson shook his head, moving around her to the opposite side of the counter. "No need to pay me. I'm happy to take a look. These are *interesting*." He took out a jeweler's loupe and set it on the counter, and then began to sift through the book that held the rings. Emma had to avert her eyes. Instead of staring—any more—she occupied herself with the contents of the glass cases that made up the front counter, crouching to examine the contents of the three displays.

The display on the far left held collectible cards—baseball, football, mostly—and some movie memorabilia. The center case was filled with antique typewriters of all shapes and sizes. And the third, far-right case held something unexpected. Blown-glass objects populated the last case, vases and tall glasses in a rainbow of colors standing beside animal sculptures and ornate bowls. The very lowest shelf of the case held small, square art pieces made of stained glass.

Emma gasped. "Who made these?"

Hudson looked up from his perusal of the jewelry, taking the loupe down from his eye. "You like them?"

"They're gorgeous. Someone local?"

He grinned, which did nothing to help her resolve to stay unabashed. "Very local. I made them all. I have a studio at my place."

"No way."

"Yes, way," he answered easily, replacing the loupe and picking up the gold belt. "You're welcome to come over and take a look anytime."

Emma let the invitation bounce right off her, unacknowledged. She strolled further from the counter, running her fingers carefully over the surface of old figurines and velvet boxes of real silverware, taking in the slightly chaotic but fascinating puzzle that Hudson had created in his shop. She was still within earshot when she heard him sigh again. Heavily.

"Well," he called out. "I have bad news. Though all of this seems to date back to somewhere in the 1920s, I'm afraid it's all costume jewelry, and none of it particularly sought after. You might get close to a thousand out of the whole lot if you find the right auction and buyer, but by the time you pay fees and maybe shipping, you'll be lucky to get two-thirds of that. Unless you have some special provenance that makes one of these unique—say, a photo of an important figure wearing one of these items—they're nice, but not a jackpot."

Emma walked back up the counter, peering over the opened books. "That's a shame. I was hoping something in here was my golden ticket to financing some of the repairs up at Cliffside."

"Not your week for the winning numbers, I'm afraid," Hudson said, a sympathetic expression flicking across his features.

"Thanks for looking at them." Emma closed each book up and packed them gently into her bag, now thinking ahead about how she'd have to tell Pip and the others that not only had she not flirted with the handsome antique store owner, but that their treasure trove was a bust.

He seemed to hesitate, as though he wanted to say something but had thought better of it. He watched her intently as she placed the last book in her bag, and he opened his mouth again, only to close it.

Emma smiled at him, curious. "Did you want to keep them?"

"No, no," he said, raising one hand. "I mean, if you want to leave them for consignment, I'll put them out for sale. And I won't charge you any consignment fees. But that wasn't what I was going to say."

Emma waited, expectant.

"Since my studio invite hint didn't land, I was wondering if you might like to go to dinner with me. There're a couple new places here in town you probably haven't tried if you just came back." Once the words were out, he shoved both of his sleeves up in what Emma could only guess was a nervous gesture, bracing both hands on the counter in front of him and leaning on the heels of his hands.

Emma had the forearms—*forethought*—to stop herself from staring, this time. She considered it a personal improvement in the alarmingly sudden social awkwardness that she'd developed since returning to Haven. Her reply rushed out, though, and she stumbled over her words. Hudson, too, cut in with a bumbling reply that made for a tangle of talking over one another, each of them trying to placate the other.

"I appreciate the offer, but—"

Hudson held up a hand. "Oh, yeah. Of course. You're busy with the house, and—"

"—bad timing, but maybe sometime after I get the major work done—" Emma's heart was in her throat.

"—if you ever wanted to, you could just stop by here. I wouldn't invite myself out to Cliffside, anyway, that would be…weird—"

She paused as his words trailed off. "Actually, consignment's not a bad idea." She plunked the bag down on the counter and scooted it toward him. "And you're more than welcome to come up to Cliffside."

Hudson stood up, pushing off the counter. "Really?"

"Yeah. In fact, I might be able to use your glass skills. Do you think you could recreate a single pane of stained glass to replace one that's broken in an existing window?"

He nodded, his eyes fixed so firmly on her that she averted *her* eyes. Dreamy and attentive? Too good to be true. "Of course. I did a restoration back in Maine of a church that had been storm damaged. Random panes shattered by hail. We got all their windows looking good as new—well, old."

Emma toyed with the loose straps of the bag, excitement building. "That's fantastic! I have one that needs repair. Let me—my contractor is going to rip out some of the stairs that are just beneath the window over the next week, so as soon as the dust settles on that, I can give you a call?"

Hudson leaned to snatch a business card out of a card holder perched on the counter. "Here. Store number"—he pointed to the printed phone number on the card, and then grabbed a pen from the other side of the register and flipped the card over, writing another number in broad, masculine scrawl—"and this is my cell number."

"Oh." Emma's face flushed.

"I'm not always at work, Emma." He leaned down to her height, resting his elbows now on the counter. Even though the counter separated them, something about the way he got down to eye level with her made it seem a much more intimate gesture.

"Well, thanks again," she squeaked. "I'll just be going. Thanks again."

You just said that, dummy.

He came from behind the counter and walked with her to the door, opening it for her to the bright, sunny sidewalk. He squinted out into the light, and then grinned. "Tell your aunt that I said hi."

Confused, flustered, and kicking herself just a little for declining his dinner invitation, Emma just laughed lightly. "Will do!"

Then, she was out the door and onto the sidewalk. She made a sharp right turn to begin her walk to Atkin's hardware—and then barreled straight into Pip, who was bent over at the shop window of Timeless Treasures, hands to the glass, peering inside.

"Pip!" Emma hollered once she'd managed to right herself. "What did I say about coming with me?"

"You do not own the sidewalk, dear, and besides"—she held up her cell phone, which was opened to a text message thread—"Louise just texted me that she is back at the house to take measurements for living room curtains, and there is water *pouring* from one of the second-floor bathrooms. She got the main water shut off, but it's draining down through the old tile and dripping from the ceiling in one of the downstairs bedrooms. I thought you should know."

Emma raked a hand through her hair, tamping down on the urge to wail. After a steadying moment, she pointed down the street. "Is everyone at Atkin's?"

"Nope. Lola took off in the Lashmobile for the house to try to assess the damage. Eric stopped by Atkin's and took Morgan and the kids home. They have to get Tilly ready for dance class."

"Okay," Emma said. Then, feeling the acid of panic rise in her chest and wipe away any warm and fuzzy feelings she had after her interaction with Hudson Ford, she said again, "Okay." It was almost as though she were trying to convince herself. "The contractor said he could start on Monday, so if we can just be sure the water is stopped and the extra cleaned up, we can have him fix things then."

"Are you sure? You don't want to call anyone?"

"I'm sure," Emma said, and she started down the sidewalk toward where she had parked by the courthouse. And again, she let loose a sentiment that she was absolutely *not* sure of.

"Everything is going to be fine."

***

By the time Lola, Pip, and Emma made sure the old shutoff valve was good and truly shut off in the upstairs bathroom, it took another two hours to sop up the water that had leaked from the cracked toilet , spread all over the bathroom floor, and dripped down through the crumbling grout and ancient subfloor to form a rather sizeable puddle on the floor of the bedroom directly below it.

Emma was exhausted by the time Lola called it quits and climbed into the Lashmobile, waving off Emma's offer of money for her day's work and offering Emma a hug instead.

When she and Pip were finally alone, Emma flopped onto the still-bare couch in the downstairs front living room, sprawling out in a haphazard slouch that gained her a disapproving look from her aunt. "Oh, dear, you'll curl your spine just as easy as your hair, " Pip fretted.

"Nonsense," Emma replied. "This won't do what years in an office chair should have accomplished. My spine is as straight as an arrow." But she sat up dutifully, watching as Pip gathered tchotchkes from the living room into a cardboard box.

Emma saw her pick up a ceramic angel that Emma remembered her own mother gifting to Pip one Christmas, before Emma and Morgan had begun spending summers at Cliffside.

"Hey," she said tentatively. "Mom gave you that, didn't she?"

Pip examined the little figurine, adjusting her glasses—which were bright green today, and adorned on the arms with little printed pineapples.

"Yes. You were so little when that happened. I'm surprised you remember."

"I remember some," Emma replied. "But not everything. I remember how much I loved it here, and that's part of why I agreed to take over the place. But do you know what I don't remember?"

Pip hummed, encouraging Emma to explain.

"I don't remember why we stayed so long. I don't remember where my mom and dad went while me and Morgan stayed here at Cliffside."

Pip stiffened, and Emma waited for an explanation that never came. Instead, Pip cleared her throat and said, "Yes, well, some memories are better off if they are left in the past."

"There's a lot that I'm trying to forget right now, Pip. I guess I'm looking for some good memories. I wondered if they went on grand vacations in thrilling locations. Maybe they were spies," Emma joked as she looked down at the thin fabric that covered the base of the couch she sat on, picking half-heartedly at the material.

"Spies? Ha! No. I don't know where they went. It's been so long that it's not worth fretting over. You could ask your mom if you really want to know."

Something in the way she said it made Emma's curiosity pique even more. Her mother had never mentioned the summers at Cliffside, and in fact, avoided talking about their move from Haven to Los Angeles as much as possible. "Mom says the same thing. Not worth it," Emma offered.

Pip placed the ceramic angel gently in the box with the rest of the trinkets she'd selected from around the house. "Speaking of worth, we got so wrapped up in the leak that I didn't ask. What was all the jewelry worth? Are we rich?"

Emma shook her head. "Only in personality. Everything was paste jewelry. Really old, but not going to fund any new crown molding."

Pip clicked her tongue. "Shame. What will you do with it?"

"Consign it with Hudson. I left it at Timeless Treasures."

Pip's gaze slid sideways to Emma. "And how did that go? Did he forgive you for throwing your drink on him?"

"I didn't throw it; it was an *accident*. And he didn't even mention it."

"Ohhhhh. So what did you two talk about that whole time?" The box was now full and resting on the coffee table, and Pip was pulling on her calf-high biker boots.

Emma murmured a noncommittal response, her heart fluttering as she remembered Hudson's charming half-smile when she'd first walked into his shop, how warm and strong his hand had been, how he'd looked so directly at her as she'd talked that she had felt truly seen for the first time in a long time. It was thrilling and unnerving at the same time.

After she'd walked Pip out to her truck, sending her off with a hug and a wave, Emma stayed in the front yard for a few more minutes, watching the sun slip down until it was only a filtered source of fading light between the branches of the heavy trees that surrounded the house.

In the twilight, Emma breathed in. It had been a day full of ups and downs, hurdles, and good surprises. Sure, the jewelry hadn't turned out to be the answer to her financial woes, but there had been time spent with her family, her new friends—and a spark of interest in her from a handsome new guy.

Of course, she wasn't ready for anything new in *that* department. It would be a long time before she ventured into any romantic entanglements, thanks to Troy and his screwups.

But as she walked back to the porch, sitting down on the steps to stare out into the darkening yard and listen to the music of the crickets, she found herself smiling at the *possibility* of dinner with the attractive Hudson Ford.

And maybe, just maybe, like the potential that she saw in Cliffside, the possibility was all she needed for right now.

CHAPTER TWELVE

The next day flew by in a whirlwind. Emma, left alone for a rare day at Cliffside, opened all the windows in the house (that would cooperate), took down every curtain in every unused room, upstairs and down, and then started weeding out knickknacks and furniture in the wing where her own room was located. She was sweating by the time she had finished hauling everything that she knew had to go out to the front living room, and even though her hair was pulled up into a high ponytail to keep her cool, tendrils that had escaped were sticking damply to the nape of her neck.

As she sat on a stack of crates in the living room, sipping a large glass of lemonade on her first break of the day, she sifted through her text messages. It was a habit she had gotten out of since she'd started weaning herself off her phone, and in addition to only checking her messages twice per day, she'd completely stopped checking her social media since quitting VogueThink. She no longer feared the odd text from Troy—though he had been conspicuously silent for the past few weeks—and she spent her evenings perusing wallpaper patterns and reading DIY home repair books. Balance was returning to her life, a feeling that she hadn't even realized she'd missed.

Her single email inbox was populated with restoration blog newsletters and quotes from repairmen, and not pressure-inducing deadlines and high maintenance client complaints. It was the former that she was sorting through now, mulling over two plumbing writeups. That took precedence, since the upstairs toilet needed to be fixed for good. Even before it had started leaking, mysteriously murky water would flow into the clawfoot tub in the same room when it flushed.

Emma shuddered.

Suddenly, she heard the heavy knocker on the front door bang firmly against the door. She swiped to check her missed calls, but didn't see that she'd missed anyone. She wasn't *expecting* anyone. When she peered through the peephole, the same fluttery nervousness that had suffused her yesterday restarted low in her stomach. She opened the door to see that Hudson Ford was even better looking in the bright spring sunshine on her front porch than he had been in the dim interior of Timeless Treasures.

He wore black boots, dark jeans, and a green T-shirt that made his eyes even brighter than before. His slightly-too-long hair was combed back, and it only served to highlight the angular attractiveness of his face. He carried a manila envelope in his hand.

"Hey," he said, and Emma had a moment where she storyboarded a soft-focus, slightly objectifying ad campaign featuring Hudson Ford peddling manila envelopes—and she was sure that every woman who would see it would feel just as swoony as she did right now.

What in the world had gotten into her? She'd been surrounded by attractive men in Los Angeles, but Emma had never been as affected as she had since attacking Hudson with her morning cup of joe. She could chalk it up to being free of Troy, but she didn't have the urge to suddenly join a dating app or go to a singles bar. No, there was something indefinably mesmerizing about Hudson Ford of the Endless Harbor Fords.

'Hi," she rasped back, swallowing and then clearing her throat. "Uh, what's up?"

He held up the manila envelope and shook it. "I have good news and bad news," he said. "Which do you want first?"

Emma pushed back the fine hairs that had escaped her ponytail and blew out a breath. "I'm already a hot mess, so I guess I could use some good news. Do you want to come in?"

"For coffee?" he said, grinning.

"You could leave," she deadpanned. Then, she let the smile that she'd been holding crack, and a laugh escaped. She stepped back into the foyer and held the door open for him. Once he stepped inside, it was like she'd let a kid into a candy store. He handed her the manila envelope without explanation, and he reached out to run a hand over the chair rail that ran the length of the foyer hallway. "This mahogany," he said, wonder in his voice. "It could use a good refinish, but it's beautiful."

Emma looked up, pointing above them "All the crown molding is original too. Sadly, some of the ceiling rosettes are cracked and need replacing, but a lot of the original trim is still good. You woodwork in addition to glassblowing and antiquing? Seems like you need your own British television series. Solve some murders in a sleepy coastal town."

Hudson let out a laugh of his own. "No. I do not woodwork. I just know a lot about these period houses by nature of all the things that come out of them. There's a lot of history in these old girls." He patted the chair rail.

Emma gestured for him to follow her to the kitchen, and once he was seated—and had declined coffee with a smirk that was half annoying and half magnetic—Emma began to peel open the manila envelope. Inside was a check for two thousand dollars.

She gasped. "What is this?"

"Turns out one of those rings was worth something. I sorted out everything you left with me yesterday, and started researching the individual pieces. There was an Elli Winslow ring in there that was from 1918, and even though the jewels were cut glass, the rings are rare enough that they are in demand with collectors."

Emma stared at the check, and then back at Hudson. "Wow. Thank you so much. This will really help."

"I thought so. Plus, I wanted to get a look inside this place. It's kind of an antiques dealer's dream." He shrugged. "And it's nice to see you."

The butterflies that seemed to tag along wherever Hudson Ford went did a small happy dance in Emma's stomach. Emma felt her cheeks heating. "I put a bunch of stuff in that front living room we passed. You're welcome to look around if you want to. But didn't you say you had good news *and* bad news? What was the bad news?"

"Oh, yes," Hudson said, wincing slightly. "You're new in town—or, back in town, right?"

She nodded.

"How long you been gone?" He was fidgeting, his fingers drumming against the island counter.

"Since I graduated high school."

He stood, seeming tense. "Long enough to not know the guy parked down by the end of your driveway, then."

Emma felt her eyebrows raise, and she set the envelope containing the check down on the island. "Who's down at the end of my driveway?"

Hudson shifted in his seat. "The guy's name is Ed Garfield. He's a land developer, and I hope you don't mind this sounding too judgey, but he's a real piece of work. A jerk of the highest order. Now, you've only just met me, so you have no way of knowing if he *is* a real jerk, or if I'm just telling you that because I once dated his sister or something—"

"Did you?"

“Hmmm?” Hudson was frowning, and he had begun pacing in her kitchen.

“I can never tell if you’re serious. Did you date his sister? Bad breakup?” Emma looked toward the door, wondering if Hudson the Hunk had dragged some sort of hometown drama to her doorstep.

Hudson stopped pacing and grinned. “No. I did not date his sister, if he even has one, and I am almost always joking. But, this time, the serious part buried in all the joking is that Ed really is a harassing kind of jerk.”

Emma hopped up onto the kitchen counter behind her, tired from her morning exertion. “So what’s the deal with Ed? He develops driveways?”

“Nope. He is parked at the end of *yours* waiting to pounce on Cliffside, I suspect. He’s made his way around every place in town over the last year, trying to buy up land. At first, he was grabbing for some of the farms around here, trying to persuade the farmers to sell so he could develop a ritzy gated community. He got one parcel on the east side, and it’s apparently in the works. He then moved on to the shops downtown because he wants to bring in more ‘upscale’ stores for when city-dwellers come out to buy their overpriced condos.”

“Yuck,” Emma said. “He sounds awful.”

“And he’s pushy. He saw me turn into your drive, and I think he’s just waiting for me to leave so he can come up here and try to sweet-talk you out of this house.”

“Which he wants to do what with?”

Hudson shrugged. “He said he’d put a Starbucks where my shop is, and I told him he could walk out or I would help him out of my store. I imagine he’s got plans for this place that do not involve preserving any of this.” A broad hand swept through the air, indicating the whole of Cliffside.

Emma sighed. “Well, it’s settled, then.”

Hudson’s brows raised, this time. “What is?”

“You’re staying for lunch so that creepy condo guy does not come up my driveway.”

“I am?” A bemused expression crept over his features. “How is that different than dinner? I recall you didn’t want to go to dinner with me just yesterday. Or should I stay for dinner, too, just in case Ed has some sticking power?”

Emma almost agreed—he was funny, and handsome, and seemed enamored of her house. They could tour Cliffside and maybe eat lunch in the wilds of the backyard, and it might be nice to have some company who was interested in her in that first-date, honeymoon-phase kind of way.

But then, she felt suddenly shy, and she regretted the boldness that she'd mustered to invite him to stay. Then, guilt suffused her. She wasn't even halfway through her divorce. Why in the world was she considering getting at all tangled up with this—admittedly charismatic—stranger?

"Dinner…" She said the word slowly, as though considering. How could she get herself out of embarrassing him—or herself—but backpedal out of spending too much time, too fast with Hudson?

He saved her the worry. "Or, how about this—you seem skittish about dinner. I don't know the story, but I promise the offer is not that serious. If the invitation still stands, I would love to have lunch with you. I'm happy to order something delivered, too. My treat."

Her guilt switched from inward facing to all about how odd she must seem to this man. And was she maybe being a tad extreme? She could be friends with him. Lunch was not a long walk on the beach, or a romantic candlelit dinner.

"Lunch sounds great. And in exchange for a tour of the majestic grounds of Cliffside, I will allow you"—she found herself smiling as he began to laugh—"to order Chinese delivery. That is, if Haven has progressed beyond burgers and pizza."

"Oh," he said, snatching his phone from the island, "I'll have you know that Haven has *two* Chinese restaurants, one Thai place, and a street ramen food truck that parks down by the boardwalk."

"Amazing! Honey walnut shrimp and fried rice, please."

"Yes, ma'am." Hudson had just pulled up the website for the restaurant and was tapping at his phone screen to start their order when the heavy knocker at the front door sounded once, twice, three times—forcefully.

"Wow, they're so good they are here before we order," Emma quipped, turning, and going to the arched entryway from the kitchen to the hall. "I'll be right back."

Feeling light and a little giddy, Emma didn't even think about who might be on the other side of the front door as she swung it open to let in the warm spring sunshine.

Outside stood a short, cranky-looking, balding man. He had a handlebar moustache that was going gray, and a thick, short beard that was more salt than pepper. Dressed a little unseasonably in a three-piece navy suit and tie, his shoes were shined to such a high polish that Emma could see the glint of them even through the screen door.

Feeling as though she already knew the answer, Emma asked, "Can I help you?"

As soon as she spoke, the man's expression changed from irritable to cheerful, a wide, toothy smile making the moustache curve upward. Emma was reminded of a shark—or a used-car salesman.

"Why, yes," the man said. "Ed Garfield, Enterprise Land Development. I was wondering if I could have a word with you about your plans for this property?"

With a glance back into the kitchen, where she could see Hudson still tapping away on his phone, Emma said, "Why don't I come out and speak with you?"

Ed moved back from the door, and Emma swung the screen door wide, stepping out with not a little amount of trepidation.

Ed Garfield really was a jerk.

The second Emma sat down with him in the pair of new rocking chairs on the front porch, he began to rub her the wrong way. He waved away her offer of tea or lemonade and leaned over the small side table between the rockers to say, "You are the owner, miss, uhm, Sullivan, correct?"

"Yes," she said carefully.

"No husband or other man around the house that makes the financial decisions? I saw you had a gentleman visitor come up the drive a while ago."

Emma bristled. "I don't think that's any of your business, Mr. Garfield. Can you tell me what you're here for?"

Ed sat back, taking a handkerchief out of his suit pocket, and dabbing at his sweating forehead. His eyes were narrowed, and the smile was gone. "Yes, yes. I'll get right to the point. I'm prepared to offer you twice market value for this dump if you sell it today."

Emma stood, crossing her arms. "It's not for sale."

Ed sat back in the rocker, as if settling in. "Young lady, I don't think you see the promise in this profit. You get more money to walk away with than this heap is worth, and the citizens of Haven by the Sea get a nice, new mall. This is the absolute perfect location—just outside of town, on the way to the beach—in fact, I own a few parcels around this place. Yours is the last piece of the puzzle. And I know you must be sinking a fortune into the repairs. Don't you want to stop the bleeding?"

Indignant, Emma tried her best to keep her rising temper at the audacity of this man out of her voice. Hudson had been so right. What a gratingly presumptuous man!

"I just came from LA, and there are *plenty* of malls there. Why don't you go develop things in the city?"

Ed stood then, dusting imaginary lint from his suit sleeve, and looking down his nose at her. "There are many here in Haven who agree with me that this little berg is behind the times. There is money to be made here, *Miss* Sullivan, and I'm sorry that you aren't amenable to getting your bit of it."

"I think you should leave my property, Mr. Garfield. And stay out of my driveway. Next time I—or one of my guests—sees you parked there, I'm calling the police."

He planted his feet, lifting his chin at her and clicking his tongue. "You'll find that there are a growing number of people who want the change you're protesting. And will find a way to *encourage* it."

"What does that mean?"

Hudson's voice behind her—and his hand on her shoulder—stopped Emma from giving Ed Garfield a true piece of her mind.

Ed, in true weasel fashion, simpered when he saw Hudson. "Miss Sullivan said she was the owner here. I wasn't aware that *you* were involved."

"I'm not," Hudson said. "This place belongs to Emma, but it sounds like she wants the same thing from you that I wanted when you came slithering into my shop—for you to leave."

Ed's mouth opened, and then closed, and then opened again. He appeared to think better of whatever he was going to say, because instead of arguing, he mopped his forehead one last time, shoved the handkerchief into his suit pocket, and stomped down the stairs. On the last step, his overzealous stomping was rewarded with a distinct *crunch*—and Emma leaned over the porch rail to find that Ed Garfield had thrust his shiny-shoed foot right through the last aged, wood step on the short flight down to the front yard.

As Ed swore and struggled, Hudson grabbed her by the elbow and pulled her gently back, shushing her as she tried to stifle her laughter with the back of her hand.

"Shhh, he'll hear you," Hudson said through chuckles of his own.

"Should we go down there and get him loose?"

Hudson craned to see Ed, and then shook his head. "He's out. His shoe is still stuck in the old tread, but he's free."

As Emma watched, Ed Garfield hobbled across the front lawn in one shoe, toward a sleek, red sports car. He squeezed himself into it, and momentarily, the engine revved, and he turned a half-circle on the lawn hard enough to send up a spray of grass and dirt. Then, he was off down the drive toward the main highway, kicking up gravel and dust behind him.

Hudson stepped toward the porch rail and looked over. "He left his shoe," he marveled.

"You were right," Emma said, coming to join Hudson at the rail and staring at the shiny oxford sticking up out of the step. "That guy *was* a jerk. But he won't spoil our day."

"Our day?" Hudson teased.

She rolled her eyes at him. "Are you ready for the tour, *Mr.* Ford?"

"Of course, *Miss* Sullivan. Lead the way."

As Hudson held the door for her, Emma took one last look over her shoulder at the settling cloud of dust where Ed had departed. There was a queasiness in her stomach, despite how she'd so easily brushed off Ed's visit on the surface. The renovation was tricky enough, with so much to plan for and schedule and juggle.

The last thing she needed was trouble from the likes of Ed Garfield.

CHAPTER THIRTEEN

Trouble came the very next day in a much different form than Ed Garfield. The upstairs bathroom began to gurgle ominously, and even though the water valve to the toilet had been shut off the day of the first leak, Emma found herself worried about the possibility of another flood of not-so-desirable substances.

The contractor who she'd been expecting early that morning hadn't shown up. As she paced in the upstairs hallway outside the bathroom in question, she dialed the number on his business card.

"Handy Mann's Contracting, this is Dusty Mann. Can't come to the phone, so leave a message."

The queasiness that she'd felt in her stomach the previous day when Ed Garfield had subtly threatened Cliffside returned in a higher, more unsettling wave, making her stomach roll with acid.

"Mr. Mann, this is Emma Sullivan at Cliffside in Haven by the Sea. We were going to start on some projects today, but neither you nor your crew showed up. I have a plumbing issue that I was hoping you could help with. Please give me a call back."

She hung up, took a deep breath, and looked at the pile of tools she had amassed on the tile floor by the bathtub. Various screwdrivers, wrenches, and pliers sat there, and not one did Emma know how to use. She would not call Hudson, no matter how pleasant the previous day's lunch had been nor how knowledgeable he had seemed about the various features of the house. And she would not call Lola, who she knew would come over right away, no—Emma would figure this problem out herself, at least until Dusty called her back. And then, Dusty could send one of his men over to figure this out and earn some of the rather hefty deposit she'd put down for the work to come.

Emma's phone rang, startling her out of her thinking. It was the very Mann that Emma had wanted to talk to.

"Sorry about the no-show, ma'am," Dusty said. "We had a gas leak out here at another project in Carmel, and I didn't have time to call you and let you know we'd need to reschedule."

"Oh! Oh, goodness. I hope everyone is okay."

"It's a whole catastrophe, honestly. There's fire trucks and the gas company and they've cleared a whole block."

"A fire?" Emma's heart jumped.

"No, luckily not. Now, why don't you tell me what your plumbing issue is, and maybe I can walk you through a temporary fix."

That phrase—*temporary fix*—was one Emma felt like she would be mumbling in her sleep for years to come. But she explained the gurgling that was coming from the upstairs tub, and Dusty tasked her with finding something called an "intermediate shutoff" to the bathroom—which he explained was different from the water shutoff for the toilet or the sink—just before someone shouted in the background and he hurriedly got off their call.

Left to her own devices, Emma was even more determined to solve the issue. She tied her hair up in a bandana and strapped on a tool belt she'd found in the attic, filling the belt with the tool pile that she'd left in the bathroom. She even located a plumbing scheme that seemed original to the house, in a pile of crumbling, rolled papers stuffed in a leather tube that had always resided on one of the tea room bookshelves. An hour and several visits to crawl spaces (and even the attic) later, Emma found the valve in question in an inexplicable place—sticking out of the wall in the bedroom that was on the opposite side of the wall where the tub rested. Sure enough, when she turned on the tub, even to a trickle, the valve and the pipe on either side of the rusty-looking contraption made very loud, very ominous groaning noises, and a sludgy gurgle continued for long minutes even after she'd shut off the bathtub faucet.

"This seems…not to code," she joked to the empty bedroom as she began to twist the handle of the shutoff valve. It, too, protested at first, but she flitted down to the kitchen for a spray can of olive oil, and after a spritz and a whack on the handle with the heaviest wrench from her tool pile, the valve seemed to loosen enough for her to turn it to closed. A test of the bathtub faucet yielded no water, no groaning noise, and no sludgy gurgle. Problem solved—for now. Pride swelled in Emma, and she gave the wrench a little flip in the air before she slid it back into her belt. She would call Lola now, just to tell her about the DIY win.

Downstairs, Emma heard the heavy knocker at the front door.

Not again, she thought.

As she tromped down the stairs, her tool belt making her feel fearless and a little superhero-y, she yelled at the front door, "Mr.

Garfield, if that's you, I told you yesterday that if you set foot on my property again, I would call the poli—"

Emma swung the front door open assertively, prepared to confront the land shark. But the sight she saw on the other side of the screen door was a much more unwelcome sight than Ed Garfield.

Standing on her front porch, holding a bouquet of what must have been at least two dozen blood red roses, was Troy. He looked nervous as he recognized her through the screen door, and she saw him take a step back as he did.

"What are you wearing?" he asked, pointing with the roses at her tool belt.

"What do you want?" she barked, completely unashamed of her tone. She clung to the harsh anger that filled her, leaning on it to outweigh the tiny, knee-jerk urge that had always led to reconciliation in the past. This time, she would not cave, nor fold. He could bring an entire field of roses, and all she would leave him with were the thorns. The presence of the flowers only served to irritate her more—they had been together half her lifetime, and he had *never* gotten it through his head that she did not care to be bought flowers. It seemed wasteful and frivolous to her, a fact that he ignored.

"You hung up on me. And, I-I-you aren't returning my calls. Or my texts. I had to find out you were here from the bank transactions."

Drat. There had been those pesky necessaries when she'd first arrived before she'd gotten her new account. "I think I've communicated fairly clearly through my lawyer, Troy."

He looked unusually contrite, his eyes dropping as he drew out his other hand—the one not clutching the absolute fountain of roses—and waved a manila envelope. "Yeah, I got these a couple days ago. As soon as I could get away from work—"

Emma interrupted with a short, sharp laugh. "Work? Is that what you call her now? I bet she really doesn't like that. I mean, Trish has always been high maintenance, but work? Troy, you can do better than that. Especially if you two want to spend the rest of your lives together."

He stepped toward the screen door as if to open it, but both of his hands were full. "Just let me come in, Emma. We can talk this out. I know this is my fault—I drove six hours to get here to tell you that. I take half the blame, at least. But wrecking our marriage? Quitting your job? This isn't like you."

Emma pushed open the screen door and stepped halfway out, causing Troy to stumble back the step he'd taken. She stared at him, at the way his lean face and angular jaw caught the light on the porch, at the beseeching eyes that had always convinced her to come back in the past. Her voice wavered slightly as she spoke, but she was proud of how strong she sounded, how sure.

"You don't know anything about me, Troy. Really, you don't. I have been an accessory for you since we were kids—just like the fancy cars, the big house, and the Hollywood friends are now. Just like Trish is—and just like you are for Trish. Go enjoy your costume parties together. You're both really good at dressing up like decent human beings."

He tried to hand the roses off to her, but she crossed her arms, refusing to take them. He set them down at her feet, instead, kneeling beside them, putting a hand on her knee as she stood in front of him. "Please, Emma, I love *you.*"

The depth of this man's delusions...

Emma stepped back, fumbling at the screen door handle, and yanking it open enough to back into the opening. Troy crawled forward, the manila envelope still in his hand, huge, blubbering sobs beginning to well up from his chest. "Please, Emma, don't. Everyone knows you left, and it's *humiliating*. I'm so sorry about Trish. I broke it off with her the minute she started thinking that she could replace you—we haven't spoken in a week. I'm alone at the house, my mom and dad say they won't pay for my legal fees, and I just—I just—just *come back where you belong*."

Emma shuffled back into the foyer, clicking the lock on the screen door, and looked down at Troy as though seeing him for the first time. It was, as always, all about his discomfort, his embarrassment, and his feelings. He wasn't sorry that he had cheated on her with Trish—the way the attention would have centered on him in the situation would have fed his ego endlessly. Sneaking around would have made him feel important. And the way Trish would have likely begged him to leave Emma would have made him feel like the star in his own movie. The same feeling he was always trying to capture with his in-crowd and body image obsession.

But there was nothing that could fill the hole that was inside of Troy. There was no pure and simple love, nor any collection of friends, lovers, and possessions that would make him feel whole. That was a feeling that he would need to cultivate for and in himself. And Emma didn't think that he was likely to do it. No, he was always trying too hard to fill that emptiness with material possessions and the adulation (and envy) of others. If losing her had not thrown him into a serious bout of self-reflection, two things were apparent—first, that she and their marriage had never been as important to him as it had to her. And second, that she was no different to him than the latest model of Lexus. He only cared about her insofar as she made him look good. And without her, he risked looking bad. Flawed. At fault.

Nowhere in her did she harbor the desire to forgive him, to make up, to accept any part of the responsibility for his selfish, childish actions. He was spoiled beyond reason, and no one could save him from himself at this point.

Still on his knees on the porch, he reached his empty hand up and splayed it on the screen. The roses behind him were being crushed under the tips of his shoes.

"Go home, Troy. If you leave now, you can be back in LA before it's dark."

And with that, she slammed the heavy wooden door in his face.

CHAPTER FOURTEEN

Emma made it to the kitchen just in time to see the giant paint bubble on the ceiling burst, sending murky water full of old plaster and goodness knows what else cascading down over the dining room.

She shrieked and jumped back, her brain unable to comprehend how in the world this much water could gather from upstairs without her knowing it.

The bathroom.

Emma shed the tool belt on the kitchen floor, grabbed her phone from the island—thankfully dry—and sprinted upstairs. To her surprise, she flung open the faulty bathroom's door to find that the tub, floor, and toilet were all sitting silent—and dry. She was already amped up and in complete turmoil because of Troy's impromptu visit, but the sound of water trickling actively downstairs amped up her adrenaline another ten notches, and she wracked her brain for what to do next. She couldn't very well turn off a shut off valve if she didn't know where the water was coming from.

Then, she remembered the plumbing schematic. Within minutes, she had shut off the main water valve to the house, and the water pouring down onto the floor slowed from above to a trickle, and then drips, and then nothing at all. The next order of business was to get the mop and bucket from the storage closet and begin mopping up the small lake that had formed where her dining room table was.

As she mopped, she cradled her cell phone between her ear and shoulder, waiting for Dusty Mann's number to ring through. Her chest was tight with anxiety as she swiped the ropey threads of the mop over the floor, wrung them out in the yellow bucket, and returned to slop up more water. She hadn't even stopped to see if Troy had left, or if he was still lurking out on her porch with his pathetic excuses, ready to "communicate" through lingo of his people—narcissistic scumbags.

This time, Dusty's voicemail didn't pick up. Emma got a three-tone alert, and then a robotic voice informed her that the number she had been trying to reach was disconnected or no longer in service. Cold fear washed over her. She left the mop leaning against the wall in the kitchen and strode to the front door, throwing it open to check if Troy was still on the porch.

He was gone.

She checked the number for Dusty and dialed again, only to get the same message. She called his office number, but there was no response, not even from the brash secretary who had arranged all the scheduling for Emma's upcoming renovation. She pulled the phone away from her ear and stared at it in disbelief. She had just talked to him.

Before she could decide what to do, a notification popped up on the screen. At first, Emma didn't click for the full message, still caught up on what to do about Dusty. But something made her brush her thumb over the notification that said, "Alert: Any more than four separate cash withdrawals in a single billing statement..."

The full message opened. The rest read, "...will incur a five percent withdrawal fee. Thank you for your business, and we look forward to continuing to service your home equity line of credit."

Frantic, she logged into her banking app and brought up the home equity line that she had taken out against Cliffside to fund the renovation. The hefty sum—$100,000 at its start—now read "$10,000 available." Several withdrawals had been made at banks across the state, the last one being down by the Mexican border.

Emma's heart sank. How stupid could she have been? Dusty had not run up any red flags on the background check nor Better Business Bureau checks she'd run, and the references she'd checked for him all had glowing things to say about him. So when he'd requested she share the credit line info with him so that he could purchase a list of items she'd approved, she hadn't thought anything of it.

Until now.

The temptation of $90,000 must have been too much for him. And it was too much for Emma to even think about losing. There was no way she could renovate Cliffside with only ten thousand dollars.

Trying to breathe nice and slowly, Emma logged out of her new account and logged into her old, shared accounts page, where the accounts that she and Troy had utilized in the past were held. There was a joint investment account, and she could just liquidate half of that and replace the money in the equity line. And then she would call the police. And then, Dusty Mann would go to jail.

Emma took another deep, slow breath.

The balance of the investment account was $4.98. It had been transferred to a new account three hours ago.

Emma sank to the floor of the foyer, holding onto the edge of the front door for support. Troy had taken all that money before he'd come here, begging her to come back. Everything in her felt betrayed all over again, fresh pain stabbing through her chest.

Above her, she heard a knock on the doorframe of the screen door. She looked up through eyes welling with tears to see that a man wearing a Haven by the Sea Sherrif's uniform was standing at her door. It had been a chaotic day, but the sight of the police officer still startled her.

"Emma Sullivan?" he asked shortly.

She nodded, but then realizing he might not be able to see her through the screen, she said, waveringly, "Yes? That's me." She'd gotten so used to answering on the phone and at the door because of the stream of activity surrounding her new ownership of Cliffside, that it didn't even occur to her that she might be in some sort of trouble.

The man slapped a bright pink slip of paper against the screen door, slipping it between the middle divider and the screen, where it stuck like a solicitor's flyer.

"You're being served a citation for failure to provide adequate fall protection on a jobsite. Pay at the courthouse within thirty days, or you will be assigned a court date if you wish to dispute. Correct the safety issue within ten days, or all construction permits will be revoked and all fees associated forfeited."

Emma gasped. "You can't be serious."

The cop leaned in closer to the screen, pulled down his aviator glasses, and looked sternly at her through the dusty mesh of the door. "Ma'am, there's a shoe embedded in your front porch step. I nearly fell over it myself."

Hot anger bubbled in her. "*He* sent you, didn't he?"

The cop straightened and didn't answer. As he turned and jogged down the steps, Emma followed him out, stopping at the top of the porch steps to yell at his retreating back.

"You tell Ed Garfield that nothing is going to get me to sell to him. And he can play these little games all he wants, but I am not going anywhere. I am *not going to quit!"*

The cop stopped midway to his cruiser and turned back to her, putting his hands on his hips. He stared at her for a long moment from behind his sunglasses, and then he spit into the grass, waved at her, and walked the rest of the way to his car.

“And you don’t scare me!” she hollered. “I worked in advertising in Los Angeles!”

The cop cruiser kicked up decidedly less dust than Ed’s sports car had, but the dust was still what Emma blamed for the flood of tears that came as it dipped out of sight, descending her driveway to the highway below.

CHAPTER FIFTEEN

The police took her theft report over the phone, but Emma was so wary after her run-in with Ed's buddy-buddy cop friend that she told the woman on the phone that she would be down the next day to get a paper copy of the filed document. Another call to the bank, who was kicking her fraud claim up the ranks to their corporate office because of the amount that had been stolen, and Emma had spent a good two hours on the phone, pacing the halls of Cliffside.

Emma needed to get out of the house—and now. She felt as though she were suffocating, overwhelmed by the cascade of bad luck that had piled on over the past days. After mopping the rest of the kitchen floor and leaving a pleading message with Lola—her pride stinging—Emma showered and changed, deciding to take Pip up on her standing offer of dinner at the new 55+ place. Her aunt answered on the first ring, and she was delighted that Emma would be on her way.

The drive was only about thirty minutes up the coast, and Emma tried to relax and enjoy the scenery as she coasted toward Pacific Cove Gardens, Pip's new community. She couldn't quite get Troy's visit, Dusty's theft, or the power-move ticket from Ed Garfield out of her head, and so much of the natural beauty of the curving route was lost on her. Before she knew it, she was turning into the Gardens, and the gateman was waving at her, smiling broadly. She gave Pip's new address, and he buzzed her in.

The gates had been impressive, ornate, and flanked with towering palms, giving the impression of an old Hollywood estate rather than a 55+ community. But once inside, Emma could see that it was a geriatric's paradise—she parked in front of the main office and community clubhouse, feeling as though she had left California completely for the deck of a cruise ship. The office was made of driftwood colored siding, built low, and featured rope accents and life preservers mounted around the outdoor lights. A block wall rose on the far side of the building, and there was an ornate mural painted on it that showed a beach and the ocean, surfers and beachgoers scattered throughout.

Smiling at the kitsch despite her awful day, Emma climbed out of her car and went to check out the inside of the clubhouse, where Pip had asked her to meet. Inside the office, it looked even more like a Carnival cruise had exploded. Once past the front desk—another smiling staff member there to direct Emma to the hot tubs—Emma took her time walking through the halls, mentally listing all the things Pip had gained with her move.

Fitness classes.

Group swimming.

Food Truck Fridays.

Bingo.

Shuffleboard Tournaments.

Golf Cart Parades.

Ice Cream Socials.

Group trips to live theater.

Regularly scheduled trips to Salinas and the casinos, to nearby malls and museums, and the library.

It sounded like a lot of fun if Emma was being honest. A lot more fun than the mess she'd gotten herself into. After fifteen minutes of scoping out all the amenities that the community center had to offer, and fending off a half-dozen invitations to join a pickleball game or jump into a horseshoe match, Emma followed the directions she'd been given to the sauna and hot tub section of the facility. It was there that her day got both worse *and* better.

Emma pulled open the door to the hot tub room not expecting anything except to find her aunt—but instead, what she found was Pip *and* some company, and they were locked in a tangle, arms around one another, kissing for all they were worth.

Emma stopped, froze, and then let out a short, surprised scream.

Pip and Bill sprang apart, and all three of them looked at one another in shock. After a minute, Bill turned, grabbed his cigar out of an ashtray that was set at the edge of the hot tub, and drew on it heavily before puffing the thick smoke out into the humid air.

"Hey, kid," he said plainly. "We weren't expecting you—were we?"

Pip looked sheepish, She had obviously not warned Bill that Emma was coming. Emma laughed—a quiet chuckle at first, but then a laugh that grew to a full-blown belly laugh. All the tension of the day drained out as she laughed, and as Pip and Bill joined in. At the end of the laugh, though, Emma found herself wracked with sobs, sinking down onto a nearby bench that sat between hot tubs so that she wouldn't plop down onto the wet pool decking.

She heard splashing, and Bill and Pip were beside her in moments. The whole story about Dusty and Troy and the ticket came rushing out of her, and Emma didn't even care that Bill was there, listening. In fact, it was kind of nice. The gruff cabbie reached over every few minutes and patted Emma's back soothingly, but he didn't interject with any advice while she was spilling her tale—which she appreciated, still being heavily embarrassed about letting herself be scammed by Dusty.

Once she was done talking and her sobs had calmed to soft hiccups, Emma looked over at Pip to find her aunt's own eyes full of tears. 'Oh, honey," Pip said. "That all sounds awful. But the police are working on the jerk who stole your money, right?"

Emma nodded.

"And Troy is gone, right?"

"Along with more of my money, yes," Emma confirmed acidly.

"And how are you supposed to comply with the citation, so your permits don't get revoked?" Bill asked, his face thoughtful.

"I don't know!" Emma wailed. "The guy just dropped the ticket and left."

"I have a buddy upstate in building code. I'll give him a call for you," he reassured.

"Thanks, Bill." Emma sniffled, feeling embarrassed, as though all she had done lately was move from giggly highs to sobbing lows. It was downright exhausting. Cliffside was supposed to have been a fresh start, not a new albatross to add to her already bird-ridden necklace of misfortunes.

"Now," Pip said, standing. "Let's go dry off and get dressed, and we can grab some food and talk about it all some more. Sound good?"

Emma nodded, but the shook her head. "Actually, I think we shouldn't talk about it at all."

Pip's expression seemed uncertain, and Emma pressed on. "I haven't come here to talk about my troubles or about the house. I've come to see you, Pip, and I'd rather spend the evening having some fun."

Pip pulled Emma in for a hug and Emma could feel Pip nodding against her shoulder. "That sounds good, dear. We're here for whatever you need."

When she pulled away, Pip's eyes had a mischievous sparkle in them. "My new neighbor is going waterskiing in the buff tomorrow.

It's a whole group thing. Why don't you stay the night and come with me in the morning?"

Emma felt her eyebrows raise. "Pip! Uh, I'd rather not."

Pip's face fell in disappointment. "Oh, ok. Well, don't say I didn't try." She turned to the man standing next to her. "Bill, what did you decide?"

"Pip, no way am I risking cartwheeling across the surface of the ocean like a skipped rock if I'm in my birthday suit. This is one adventure you will have to fly solo on."

"You two, I swear," she fussed. "No fun at all."

Bill grinned at Emma. "We're boring."

"I wish," Emma retorted as Bill and Pip gathered their towels, and Pip her bag. "I'll take boring any day over being robbed—twice!—and slapped with a ticket for an unsafe construction site."

"Let's go forget our troubles over margaritas!" Pip did a little shimmy dance as she moved toward the hot tub room doors.

That sounded great to Emma.

***

It turned out that Pip's offer of margaritas had been an excuse to show off her new frozen margarita machine, which she swore to Emma was not used for boozy smoothies all the time—no, Pip swore that she had plans to make real, healthy things in the slushy maker at some point in the near future. But for tonight, it had held a concoction of tequila, limeade, and sweet and sour mix that was helping Emma to relax all her cares away.

Bill left after a relaxed dinner of nachos—which he made skillfully, and Emma scarfed down gratefully—and Pip and Emma were left to their own devices.

"I don't know what to do, Pip," Emma said once they were alone. "Troy, the money, everything. I was getting the hang of things, feeling good on my own. Now, I'm just lost. Should I sell Cliffside to Ed and go back to LA? Not to Troy, of course, but to marketing? I just feel like ever since I took over Cliffside, I've been cursed. "

"Hush," Pip admonished. "There's no such thing. You've just hit a low streak, that's all. Your luck will change soon. And maybe you just need to look on the bright side, dear."

Emma slurped at the bottom of her second margarita. "There's a bright side?"

Pip nodded. "Look, I can't tell you what to do. But I can tell you that even if this was a mistake, it brought us all together again—you, me, Morgan—and when you are with family, that's worth something."

Emma set her empty glass aside. "That's true." And she knew it was—no matter how hard things got with her personal life or the work on the house, she was always happy when she thought about remaining so close to Pip, Morgan, and the kids.

Pip grinned and hopped up to refill Emma's drink. "Have another, and you can tell me while you drink it all about Troy coming to grovel on the porch. I want *every* detail."

Emma laughed, held out her hands for Pip to press a fresh drink into, and obliged.

CHAPTER SIXTEEN

The next morning, bright and early—or, as early as she was able after sleeping off a four-margarita night in the guest room of Pip's new place—Emma went into town. Aside from her visit to Timeless Treasures after their group lunch at the diner, Emma had been so busy with the renovation that she hadn't had time to just wander around down Main and off the side streets, seeing what had changed about her hometown. After a heavy breakfast of eggs, pancakes, and bacon at Rooster's café, Emma took off walking, headed for parts of Haven unknown.

She meandered around for about an hour, and she was almost at the end of the main drag when she turned down a side street and saw a small wooden plaque hanging that simply said, "Art Supply." She thought of her old tubes of paint at Cliffside, and her improvised curtain canvas, and she was struck by a longing to go inside this new store and breathe deeply of the cut wood of the canvas frames and the heavy oiled smell of the paint tubes, run the soft, dry horsehair brushes across her cheeks. In all the renovation hubbub, she had nearly forgot about her art. Painting had always helped ease her anxiety in the past; and now, with all the chaos swirling in her new life, bleeding over from her old life, she could use some stress relief more than ever.

She had intended for the walk to clear her mind, but now it was filled with excitement—and a little sadness. Her father and the story of the Atkins art display replayed in her memory, and it pained her to know that he wasn't here for her to show this to—how Haven finally got an art store. He wasn't here so she could buy supplies and paint for him.

Inside the store, Emma's excitement grew. The place was wall-to wall art supplies, with displays of oil pastels and Prisma pencils arranged around stacks of pre-stretched canvas. There was a single register near the back, and an elderly man, tall and gangly, stooped over as he sat on a stool behind the long, wooden counter there. He looked up from the book he was reading when she came in, but didn't greet her or say anything at all.

"Hi," she said, trying to break the ice herself. "I'm just here to browse."

"Well," he huffed, his voice deep and booming, "Be sure to browse with your wallet, not just your eyes. You're the first person I've seen in here all morning, and the rent does not pay itself with browsing."

Taken aback a bit, Emma could only nod. She took a shopping basket and went from wall to wall, display to display, picking out fresh paint and brushes and even a new mixing pallet. She took everything up to the register, where the old man stopped reading, sighed, and turned to address her.

As he began ringing up her purchases, he eyed her curiously. "You paint, or is this a gift for someone?" he asked.

"I paint."

"No canvas today?" he asked, seeming to relax a bit when the total of her supplies topped a hundred dollars. He was still adding items up.

"No. I'm actually going to paint a mural on a library wall."

"What library?" He had stopped ringing and was looking at her askance now, as though she were pulling his leg.

"The library at Cliffside," she explained. "I'm the new owner. I'm restoring it."

He grunted. "Good. It's art."

She frowned, confused. "The library?"

"No, Cliffside," he said, taking out a canvas bag that said, "Greenberg Art Supply," and slipping her purchases inside. "Lots of places like that in this town, beautiful things just getting lost in the modern life."

"Are you Mr. Greenberg?" Emma asked, pointing to the bag.

"I am. Erwin Greenberg. That'll be two hundred three dollars and sixty cents." He whistled low. "I've not had an order this large in a month."

Emma handed him her debit card and squinted, considering the wisdom of telling a joke to this acerbic man. "Can I ask you something?"

"You're a customer now, so you get one question free per paying visit," he groused, swiping her card through the card reader.

He handed her back her card as the receipt for her supplies spit out in slow, noisy screeches. He tore off one copy and plonked it in front of her.

"Why was the artist afraid he might go to jail?" She watched as Erwin's mind worked on the problem as she signed the sales slip. It was a joke her dad had told her, and it had taken her a while as a kid to work the answer out. But her dad had always said that laughter could connect people, and Emma felt an unexplained pull to connect with the standoffish Erwin Greenberg.

"Ok," he said after long moments. "I'll bite—why was the artist afraid he might go to jail?"

Emma picked up her bag and put it over her shoulder. It was satisfyingly heavy with all her purchases. "Because he'd been framed!"

Erwin guffawed, once, and then smiled for a flash of several seconds. "Have fun painting your mural," he said, turning to pick his book back up. "Come back if you run out of anything."

Emma left the store, a secret smile on her lips.

Good job, Dad, she thought. *Your joke might just have worked.*

***

From the art store, Emma headed back to her car. The morning was warming up, and she had exterior work to do on Cliffside. If she couldn't fix the plumbing reliably, at least she could paint the exterior of the house. She rounded the corner by Sunnyside Diner, and nearly ran smack dab into Hudson Ford. Emma could have cried when she saw that he was carrying a huge to-go cup of coffee.

No collision happened, though, and he simply stopped and grinned at her. "Are you traumatized?" he asked waving his coffee. "I need my caffeine, even on my day off."

"I think I can push through the emotion," she joked back. Then, her ears perked up. "Did you say day off?"

"Yep."

"Big plans?"

"You're looking at 'em," he said, waving the cup.

"How would you like to come back to my antique paradise and help me paint the outside of Cliffside?" It was out before she could consider the wisdom of the ask—but when his eyes lit up, she was immediately excited as well.

"Yes! Can I—can we meet at the house?"

Emma nodded. "Sure. I'm headed back now."

"Give me fifteen minutes. I'll be at your door."

And with that, Hudson zoomed off toward his shop. Emma, feeling excitement beginning to build at the possibility of a day's completed work and some nice company, had a spring in her step as she walked back to her own car.

***

Emma and Hudson painted a good half of Cliffside before they had to take a break. She found him an excellent help, and the only issue was that he was easily distracted by the intricate architecture of the house, oohing and aahing around every corner they painted.

"Did you know," he said, bending down while they both balanced on the roof, "that Victorian era houses had slate tile roofs?" He tapped on the wooden roof tiles beneath their feet. "These were used, but were less desirable when compared to slate. If you replace this with slate, it will also last you a very, very long time."

"I did not know that," she said.

He grinned. "Now, you do."

Emma watched Hudson as he painted and pointed, extolling the virtues of the house structure while occasionally expressing remorse over the weak spots—as if they were in him instead of a house. His passion for history and preservation really shined. Emma was impressed. She had never seen the house through someone else's eyes like this, and she found that Hudson's passion was inspiring her.

"Can I tell you something?" she asked, dipping her paint brush into the paint gallon at her feet.

"Of course," he replied, carefully cutting his own paintbrush around the edge where the wall met the fascia.

"I've been pretty overwhelmed at Cliffside. I was actually about to give up, maybe sell to Ed."

"No!" Hudson said, frowning. "Please, I can't let you do that. You owe it to the house—that work of art—to see this through."

Emma set down her paintbrush. Art—that was what Mr. Greenberg had called Cliffside.

"Don't you see, Emma? Cliffside isn't just a house. We are where we live. You came from LA, right?"

She set her brush down, nodding. She was suddenly wary, unsure of how much of her story she wanted to share with Hudson.

"Does anywhere in LA really feel like home?" he asked, setting down his own brush.

After a long, quiet moment, she answered honestly, "No." It was something she had thought of previously, but the importance of it struck here. She'd spent her entire married life in a place that had never felt like home.

"But here, at this house, do you feel it? Even despite the drama, or maybe because of it—ghosts of the past, emotionally messy family, generations of stories in the walls, a million pieces that furnish the halls and hang on the walls that will speak to you of past lives. It makes you feel like maybe things aren't so bad. Everyone who has passed through these doors has lived things like us before. And they did, live. So it gives you a little perspective. Please don't give that up. "

Emma smiled at the poeticism in his description. "You know what, Hudson? You're right. I have no reliable water, but at least I am not dying of consumption."

He winked at her, retrieved his brush, and resumed painting.

Emma warmed from her stomach to her toes.

Uh oh, she thought. *I am in trouble.*

CHAPTER SEVENTEEN

"You are an angel sent from God," Emma said.

She stood in the front yard and surveyed the new steps that led from the yard to the porch. They shone with rich wood stain, and each tread contrasted nicely with the painted white of the newly restored porch spindles and railings.

"Thanks," Lola said, putting a hand on her hip and staring at the staircase herself. "It turned out nice. Real nice."

"And all reclaimed wood," Emma added, turning to give Lola a high-five. "You are a genius."

"Well, all except that one special feature," Lola said, and they giggled together. On the bottom step of the new stairs, right in the cut-out center, set in epoxy so that the top was smooth and level with the stair tread, was Ed Garfield's lost shoe.

"Yeah, that's just art," Emma cackled. "I mean, nothing like the new mural in the library, but I did my best."

Even though the budget was meager, between Lola and Emma, they had managed to get a lot accomplished in the past couple weeks at Cliffside. Lola was now a fixture at Cliffside, and Emma was dryly delighted to note that Lola was one of the only fixtures in the pace that worked reliably. She juggled helping out at the house and her responsibilities with Ethan like an expert, and Emma really admired Lola for her ability to do so.

And there were other things that were falling into place, too. Emma found that, even with her self-imposed deadline of Memorial Day approaching very quickly, the stress of finding workaround solutions to her money woes was not as much a burden as she had expected. Morgan and the kids had come every weekend, as promised, and Eric had tagged along, power tools in hand. New paint and curtains in all the bedrooms, sanding down and refinishing the hardwood floors, and new ceiling fans to circulate air in the house made slow but very noticeable differences. It was possible they might be able to host people soon, in order to start the place earning.

Except…

"Now, the pipes." Lola's tone was tentative, and Emma knew why—the plumber who had come out to assess what had happened with the flood of the kitchen from upstairs had said that the entire ceiling of the dining room would need to be torn down in order to truly know what had happened that night, as well as prevent any more repeats of the bizarre leak that had started when Emma had simply turned off the water in the upstairs bathroom. Lola and Emma had torn down just the section of ceiling where the water had flowed, locating the busted pipe—Lola thought it had burst from age and the water pressure redirect when Emma had turned off the water valve that night—and Lola had cut the pipe and put in adapters and a new, short length to replace the split section.

Emma was still afraid to use the whole-house water, turning it on only to take short, cold showers or run the toilets, and then she would dash to the main shutoff to turn it off again before any other catastrophes happened. She had big, five-gallon water jugs delivered, and she used those to drink and cook and brush her teeth. Hand-washing clothes was a pain, but Emma was slowly learning about all the things she could live without—and in some ways, it was making her previous big-city, fancy-house life seem like even more of a sham.

It was at least something of her own, something untainted by her time with Troy and his—or his parents'—money.

"We can't afford to rip all that out," Emma said. "After fixing up the dining room, the bedrooms in my wing, and the living room and tea room, there's nothing left over for hiring that plumber."

"Well, about that…" Lola trailed off, and then looked over at Emma, frowning. "Promise you won't get mad if I tell you something?"

Emma blanched. "Tell me how you'd react if your son started out a conversation that way."

Lola laughed, and the pair of them started up the porch steps to get out of the sun, settling into the rocking chairs where Emma still had the smallest, sourest memory of the annoying Ed Garfield talking down to her. Ugh. She was glad she hadn't seen him since she'd kicked him off the property. Every time she went to town, she half expected him to pop out from around a corner, twirling his moustache like some silent-film villain.

Lola must have picked up on Emma's train of thought because she said, "Mad or not, unless you will agree to my solution of tracking down Dusty Mann and punching out a few of his teeth as revenge for stealing you blind, you'll have to agree to this other plan I worked out.

I bartered some labor time for the plumber for *his* labor on *your* project. So, if you can come up with the money for the hard supplies only—any pipe he needs, glue, new drywall, whatever—he will do the actual work for free."

Emma sat up in her rocking chair, gripping the arms. "Lola, no! You need that time with Ethan. That's not fair. Just because I'm running out of reno money does not mean that I'm any kind of charity case."

Lola waved away Emma's concern, digging her phone out of the back pocket of her jeans and swiping around it before showing the screen to Emma. "Nah. You need a kitchen that actually works all the way. And *hot* water on *all the time*. And if the guy sees I'm serious, he'll let me apprentice with him, which will help me if I decide to take the state license exam. It's a win-win.

"Plus, see, Ethan wants to go to this game coding camp this summer, and it's two whole weeks. So I'll go work for the plumber then." Lola turned the phone back to herself. "It's the first time Ethan's wanted to go away for this long. It helps that Daniel is going. They really hit it off."

Emma could see the mix of sadness and joy in Lola's expression. She felt a pinch in her chest as she thought about how she might have missed out on her window to feel this—this swirl of emotions for another person, one made from a piece of you, one who was so closely tied to your heart. Emma always felt bitter when she wondered if she'd spent the best years of her life with Troy, who'd squandered her years the way he tossed away his parents' money. And then, she would wonder why in the world she had stayed so long—and wasted her own time.

"You're a good mom, Lola," Emma said.

Lola chuckled. "You said that before. You should actually meet him one of these days."

"Morgan talks so much about what a great kid he is, I feel like I have," Emma replied. "But bring him with you next time you're here and he's off school. Or to the party—the soft opening. That's next week."

Lola nodded. "I will."

"And Lola?" Emma studied the petite redhead's profile, and she noticed that Lola's face was uncharacteristically somber.

"Hmm?"

"Thank you. For helping me, and for being my friend. You didn't know it when you showed up here, but I really needed a friend."

Lola reached out and grabbed Emma's hand, squeezing it in hers. "Sometimes, we don't know we need people until people come into our lives," she said, her eyes going misty. "When I came up here to check out Cliffside when you first arrived, I just thought I was coming up to see some vintage baseboards, maybe get a few side jobs to keep me and Ethan covered for money in between other work. I didn't expect that I would get to know you and Pip and Morgan and the kids the way we have. I think it's us who owes you all a word of thanks."

Emma squeezed back. "You're right," she said. "Sometimes you never know you need people until they come into your life."

As they sat in contemplative silence, Emma couldn't help but think of laugh lines around mesmerizing green eyes, random bits of knowledge about the historical facets of the trinkets and details in Cliffside itself, and about how Hudson Ford had come out onto her porch to defend her from Ed, climbed up onto her roof to help her paint without an ounce of hesitation, and would now be coming to her soft opening—the thought of which made the same familiar butterflies take flight in her stomach.

Was Hudson Ford someone who Emma needed in her life?

CHAPTER EIGHTEEN

"Where did she even get those giant scissors?" Tilly looked up at Morgan, whispering. "And can I have a pair? Please?"

"No, dear." Morgan's voice was calm and even, but she looked across at Emma and mouthed, "*Thanks a lot.*" Out loud to her daughter, she said, "Now, stay still and out of the frame so I can take Aunt Emma's picture."

Emma held back a laugh. At least Tilly had moved on from dreaming of moving to dangerous major cities to coveting large, dangerous objects. Maybe it was a step in the right direction. One could lock up a pair of gigantic scissors, but there was no protecting Tilly fully from the glittering sprawl of Los Angeles and all the potential pitfalls it contained. Emma smiled, keeping it in place until her lips began to shake. She knew all too well how someone could get lost in the City of Angels.

It was now three days until their soft opening, three days of Emma checking and rechecking her email for any new news from her divorce lawyer or her real estate agent, who'd finally listed the Los Angeles house. She'd had to go back to her habit of turning off her phone, she had been so obsessively checking for new messages. She kept looking through the online listings of the house, scrutinizing the pictures, wondering if there was something in the property or the staging, the amenities, or the listing price, that was causing radio silence when it came to offers on the luxury abode.

And as far as the divorce was concerned, she knew that Troy had his papers. He'd had them with him the day he'd come begging her to come back to him. Why he hadn't just signed them and gotten it all over with was beyond Emma. It made her bristle to think that it might be one last grab for control—the same way that he'd taken away her financial ability to renovate Cliffside after Dusty had taken her equity line money—and she sat in anger, upset but not surprised. He had been so used to getting his way their entire life that it was probably turning his world on its axis just being told no about something.

She did wonder at one thing he had said while he'd been on his knees on her porch, groveling in hopes of saving himself from being humiliated by the consequences of his own actions.

My mom and dad say they won't pay for my legal fees.

It was something Emma had been chewing over in her mind since he had blurted it out. Troy's mom and dad had been the king and queen of enabling their son's horribly spoiled personality since birth, and to think that there was somewhere that they would draw the line was shocking. Not only had they never drawn one before—Emma assumed that they would want to protect Troy in any asset split that might result from their divorce. But to leave him to his own devices, instead of using the high-powered attorney that she would place her own money on that Mom and Pop Adams had on retainer? Another mystery that she would probably never have the answer to.

As of this morning, Emma couldn't spare much time at all for thinking of Troy, the divorce, the house, or her ex-in-laws, because Cliffside had a guest. Dan Larson, last-minute business tripper and writer for *Sleek Travel* magazine, had needed a place to stay in Haven by the Sea. In his words, "Somewhere quiet where he could get work done." So he had called Emma, and even though they were not supposed to be officially guest-ready for several days, she had extended an invitation for him to be the first to overnight at Cliffside, which he had accepted. The soft opening party was tonight, and Emma just knew that Dan would have nothing but rave reviews for the changes she and her friends had made to make Cliffside a magical step back into the heyday of the historic house.

Now, Dan was standing next to Emma, having been coerced after his arrival into a first-guest commemorative photo. Morgan and Tilly, who had arrived early to help get the food ready for the soft opening tonight, had been roped into photography duty.

Emma was on cloud nine. Not only did Cliffside have its first guest, but he was the kind of guest with connections, and a ready audience hungry for new travel experiences. Dan could spread the good word about the bed and breakfast. And, on top of that, if all went according to the plan in Emma's head, the house sale would soon go through, and she would have money again. Money for things like electrical work and landscaping and big, new canvases that she could use to paint new pieces—just for Cliffside.

The room they were standing in had turned out beautifully. The four-poster bed had been sanded down and the stain restored. The heavy velvet drapes around the bed were newish, having been salvaged from dozens of yards of red velvet that Pip had bought to make a Thanksgiving float out of her truck one holiday—but had stored in the attic when a visiting Frenchman had become smitten with her and asked her to fly to Paris with him for Turkey Day, instead.

The walls were a soft, eggshell cream color, and Emma was soothed just being surrounded by it. She hoped their guest—Dan from *Sleek Travel*—loved it as much as Emma did. She took a steady breath, trying to calm herself so that she didn't come off as overexcited. She didn't want travel suave, road scholar Dan to think that she and the rest of her friends were clueless when it came to running a B and B. So she counted slowly from one to ten in her head, took deep, slow breaths, and thought *professional, calm, and confident—professional, calm, and confident* over and over in her mind.

"Ok, ready!" Morgan shouted. "Three second timer. One, two…"

Flexing the handles of the aforementioned giant scissors, Emma waited until Morgan called, "Three!," and then she cut the thick red ribbon that she had stretched across the doorway leading to the first bedroom of the renovated wing of Cliffside.

It was a perfect day. Nothing could spoil it.

Just as Morgan's phone flashed, the ceiling above Emma and Dan opened up, and the rest happened in what seemed like slow motion. The break in the drywall over the top of them caused a shower of wet plaster and water to *whoosh* all over Emma and Dan. After it hit them, the torrent hit the floor, and then kept cascading across the carpet like a small tsunami. Morgan shrieked and jumped back from the collateral splash. Tilly shrieked and rushed forward, catching the downward force of the water now running freely from the ceiling. She slid under the water at just the right angle—and the strength of it ripped the sequined scrunchie right out of her ponytail. She shrieked again in delight and twirled in the water as it continued to empty from some unknown—but seemingly endless—supply in the heavens.

"This is amazing!" Tilly said, starting to practice her tap dancing under the deluge.

This is the worst! Emma wanted to scream. She was frozen in place, her mind scrambling for a solution—what to do first? All she could do was stand stock-still in indecision, locking eyes with Morgan, who looked equally paralyzed.

Dan was moving, however. He seemed to turn in molasses-like degrees, his face stricken as he slow-lunged toward where his luggage was. But he wasn't fast enough. The surge of water hit his laptop bag full-force, and the bag was instantly saturated with a mixture of drywall particles and dirty water.

Emma could do nothing but stand there, shock still numbing her.

As the water slowed from above, which might have taken two seconds or two hours, Emma wasn't sure, Emma turned to look at Dan, who was standing over his now-open laptop bag, his computer out. There was the smell of something electronic burning as he stabbed at the power button over and over—but nothing happened. Fury fell over his features, and he whirled to face to Emma.

A small poof of dense, black smoke was the outcome of his last stab, and it puffed out of the laptop fan vent like the last dying burp from an old car's exhaust. Emma couldn't suppress a giggle. It was completely inappropriate, but the laugh escaped her before she could hold it back.

She looked around at the ruined room—the whole *situation* was just cosmically ridiculous. Not even something she could have made up if she tried.

"What in the heck kind of place are you running here? You think this is some kind of joke? Huh?" Dan shook his computer. "My entire trip's writing is on this machine, so you'd better hope that my file backup is working or you will be hearing from the *Sleek Travel* legal department!"

Emma floundered for a response. *Sorry* didn't seem to cut it, and he was still standing there as if he expected her to have some kind of clever solution for the fact that the ceiling had come crashing down in some kind of comedic "I Love Lucy" setup. She certainly couldn't turn back time to stop it from happening, so the only thing they could do was face it, head-on, and start cleaning up.

Emma turned back to Morgan. Her sister was still holding her phone, the camera pointed toward Dan and Emma. In her shock, there was only one thing Emma could think of asking. "Did you get the pic?" she blurted.

Morgan burst into laughter, and Emma fought not to burst into tears. Tilly was going unnoticed in the whole fiasco, and so she sat in the middle of the inch-deep water, as happy as could be. What a story she would have when she made it home—an experience that none of her siblings would have. She was grinning ear to ear.

Dan stuffed the ruined computer into his laptop bag and plonked the carry strap over the handle of his rolling luggage. It was clear from his narrowed eyes and grim-set lips that he was fuming. "This is *unacceptable.*" He rolled to the door of the bedroom. "I will be posting this on *all* of my social media, contacting the local news, and writing an article about my experience at Cliffside. This place will be *ruined.*"

And with that, he left. Emma heard him squashing wetly down the hall, his shoes obvious waterlogged.

As silence settled over the room, Emma looked around. So much water had fallen so fast that much of her hard work had been reversed, and the finished room had been instantly ruined. They would have to start over again. Disbelief and paralysis gave way to desperation—the house money was not promised, she was still stuck in her marriage, and she didn't have the money to fix this room. They could close it up, but she envisioned the same catastrophe happening in every one of the already-prepped guest rooms, the ancient pipes deciding that it was just time to give up, room by room, in the very wing she had decided to start her redecorating in.

Emma caught a sob on a hiccup, trying to choke back both.

Maybe the ceiling in her own room would give way one night while she slept, *wooshing* her out of her bed and carrying her all the way to the ocean. Where she could live as a mermaid without a care in the world.

No toxic ex-husbands who wouldn't accept the end.

No scheming contractors who cleaned you out and left you high and dry without the means to fund your dream.

No need for band-aid fixes in a house that deserved to be lovingly well-restored so that the memories made here would not be forgotten, lost to decay and the passage of time. All she needed was for the Los Angeles house to sell, and for Troy to relinquish his half of the house profit and her half of their joint account, and her life would be so much more financially secure.

But what if that doesn't happen? Ed Garfield's offer—and Hudson's arguments against it—swam in the back of her mind.

Emma walked over to Tilly, who reached up a hand. Emma took it, held it, and plonked down beside her niece in the dirty water.

Laughter rang out—loud, boisterous, and undeniably Pip. Emma whipped her head up to see her aunt doubled over in the doorway, laughing so hard that she clutched at her stomach.

"I came to see the room," she said between gasps for breath and swipes at her brimming eyes. "But when I got here—the very second I came down the hall and into the doorway—here comes the water! Oh, you two should have seen the magazine guy's face!"

Morgan began to laugh, and Tilly laughed, and soon, Emma's crying had turned completely to laughter as well. The water around her was cold, she was now soaked through all layers of her clothing—her shoes probably ruined beyond saving—but she joined in laughing with her family.

It will be okay, she thought. *I'm okay. I have family here with me. And friends.*

Looking around the flooded room, Emma realized that nothing needed fixing that they hadn't already had experience fixing, and fixing together.

The stress and anxiety took a back seat, replaced with a sudden resolve to just get up and get past all this. She recognized in this moment that she felt happier than she had been in a long time—even despite the mess.

Emma stood and was about to start handing out cleanup assignments when, out past the hallway, she heard that joyfully dreaded sound—an engine cutting off, followed by the heavy knocker sounding on the front door.

CHAPTER NINETEEN

"Why can't I come in?" the man whined, stomping his foot on the front porch. "I'm *family*."

"Stuff and nonsense," Pip said, stomping her foot in return. Emma and Morgan crowded behind her, and Tilly had been banished to the living room until the adults could figure out what to make of this odd prodigal cousin. Emma didn't know if she could handle any more drama today—or this month, Maybe this year.

"What right do you think you have to tell any of us to 'vacate the premises?'" Pip asked, latching the screen door on the inside as the man reached for the handle. He jiggled the door with some force, but it held.

The man—mid-height, middling weight, around forty, and average in every other way, snorted as he stood there. "Why else would I show up here? And with this?" He waved a paper that was old and yellowing, and Pip unlatched the door, reached out, and snatched it from his hand when he held it out. She somehow clicked the lock back into place before he could haul the screen open and get to them.

"Give that back," the man barked. He sneered at them, looking from Pip to Morgan to Emma, wrinkling his nose at the two younger women as he took in their wet hair and clothes. "And why are you two soaking wet?"

"We were burying a body out back," Morgan said, deadpan. "Solicitor. Had to hose off the evidence. Gosh, imagine how annoyed we are with you if that's the end result of some poor sap trying to sell us a vacuum cleaner?"

"You're cute. You'll be cute when the cops escort you out of there in the next forty-eight hours."

Pip murmured as she scanned the printed page. Then, something caught her eye. "Sandra! You're Sandra's boy, Nathan? I should have known. Your mother was always a troublemaker. It looks like you are, too. Emma, call the police."

Nathan held up a placating hand, which did nothing to placate anyone. "Calm down, Aunt Pip. A little birdie down my branch of the family tree told my mother that you had gone to an assisted living facility, and that you had abandoned this place. Now, my mother asserted her rights over this house years ago, as you can see by *that* paper. And if you truly have moved on from the house, then it is rightfully her inheritance. And as she is in the hospital and unable to come claim it—"

Pip crumpled up the paper and tossed it between her hands as if she were about to practice her softball pitch. "You thought you would use her comatose state as a way to grab for assets before she's even passed? Wow. You're a real peach."

Nathan scowled. "We have asserted our rights over this house!" he thundered.

"Please, spare me. You didn't come with any recent legal proof. And contesting my father's will twenty years ago does not equal 'asserting your rights over this house,'" Pip explained, throwing the paper down to the floor and kicking it to the side. Emma squashed her wet suede flat over the lump, watching as water squelched out of her shoe and made mush of the document.

Nathan practically growled.

Pip held up a finger, wagging it at the man on the porch. "And the very court case you are referencing is public record, so you won't have any trouble going down to the courthouse yourself and finding out that your mother—and now, by proxy, you—lost that claim a long time ago in due process."

Pip laughed again before she continued. "You'd never be able to handle a place like this, even if you got it. Besides, it belongs to Emma now." Pip threw a thumb Emma's way. "It's deeded and signed over. Ironclad. There's nothing you can do short of Emma willing the place to you or deciding to sell—which she ain't doing—that would get your name anywhere close to this property."

Cousin Nathan's face grew a mottled shade of purple. He swung his laser-focused, beady eyes toward Emma. She shrank a little from the force of the gaze, unused to anyone displaying such naked fury at her for no reason other than greed. And it was greed—because if dear Cousin Nathan could see the renovation costs that came along with Cliffside, he would beat a fast retreat. Emma was sure that the only thing in his head were dollar signs. And she was sure that Nathan was the type who would take Ed Garfield up on his buyout in two winks. That made up Emma's mind. Pip was right. There was no way anyone was getting ahold of Cliffside unless it was over Emma's dead body.

She thought of Hudson, and how he would smile if he heard her say that.

"This isn't over, Emma," Nathan spat. "I will see all of you in court—and then, I will enjoy kicking you out of *my* house when the time comes."

With that, Nathan turned on his heel and stomped off down the porch, yanking his small, wheeled luggage behind him.

The three of them—Pip, Emma, and Morgan—watched until he was gone down the driveway. Emma couldn't see where he had parked when he'd arrived, and she had a brief, funny flash of him simply hoofing it down the highway back into town, towing his wheeled suitcase the whole way. Maybe magazine Dan would meet up with him, and the two men could commiserate on how awful Cliffside was.

"Well," Pip said, clapping. "That didn't go as planned. Who wants margaritas?"

***

A week later, the entire Cliffside crew stood in Emma's dining room, looking up. Emma stood behind the island, closest to the stove, grinning at the spectacle of Morgan, Eric, the kids, Lola, Ethan, Pip, Louise, Carol, Bill, and the plumber (whose name was Gerald), all craning backward to stare at the new ceiling.

"Seamless," Eric said with wonder in his voice. "I cannot even see where the pieces come together."

The gathered group murmured agreement, and Gerald smiled in response. He had a wizened face that reminded Emma of an apple doll, and his eyes practically disappeared when he grinned his toothless grin. He had worked with Lola on the dining room and all the ceilings in the re-done bedrooms, toiling for a solid week. In fact, the last spackle over the seam tape had happened only this morning in the last bedroom.

Emma felt silly thinking it, but she was so happy in this moment that she could burst. Sure, they'd had to scoot back the soft opening, and their group—which had started with the simple act of Pip cajoling Emma into escaping to Haven—was a bit of a ragtag bunch, but Emma found more and more that the individuals who were coalescing around her were more genuine, caring, and loyal than almost anyone she'd been around in Los Angeles all those years. And she was spending more time with Morgan, Eric, and the kids. And Pip was having a blast at her new place—and with Bill, though he would be loath to admit it.

"The new fan is a nice touch. I guess the blessing to the whole houseful of ceiling coming out was that you could just reroute some electrical," Pip said. "And we know no one is going to get a cold, wet, surprise wakeup call."

Emma loved a good ceiling repair as much as the next homeowner, but she was most pleased with the fact that she now had running water that she was not afraid to use. "There were two other pipe sections up there getting ready to crumble to bits because of age. Just in the kitchen! And most of the rooms had a pinhole leak or two that would have washed out a future guest." Emma lifted her glass of wine in salute. "But everything up there is now shiny, new copper piping, so good old Cliffside will be ready for guests starting this Monday!"

The cheer that went up from the gathered—exaggerated by the kids to a hilarious degree—blocked out the first few knocks at the front door. Emma, laughing, shushed them all. "Morgan, take the lid off that meat and cheese tray. Lola, you can open the sparkling apple juice for the kids now. I'll be right back."

Figuring that nothing could happen again that was quite as ridiculous as the parade of absurdity that had come across her front porch in the past weeks, Emma had lost her fear of the front door knocker. What had brought Ed, Troy, the permit threat cop, and Cousin Nathan to her door all in close order had also been host to her shipment of beautiful replica Victorian doorknobs, had been the sight of the discovery of a flood of hummingbirds—who had not knocked, but had set up a series of light, musical taps on the front windows, being attracted to the combination of bright white trim and dark purple wall color on the exterior of the freshly-painted house—and had been the threshold through which her newfound family had come in, showing up again and again to help her and cheer her on and keep her company as both Emma and Cliffside rose from the ashes like a Phoenix.

Now, it brought another pleasant surprise—Hudson Ford, standing on her front porch looking like a model from a menswear catalog. He shifted from foot to foot in the exact location where Troy had stood, like something meant to erase all the unpleasant memories that Emma had of *that* particular spot. He was dressed in heavy boots, dark jeans, a white T-shirt, and a dark brown thin corduroy suit jacket with leather patches at the elbows. His hair was tousled, and he had the faintest five o'clock shadow that only served to make him look more rugged, and not unkempt, as she usually found was the case on other men.

Emma opened the door to see that he held a long, somewhat thin box in his hands and a nervous expression on his face.

"Hi!" she said brightly. "I'm glad you made it. Come in!"

He smiled and came into the foyer, giving her a short hug that made her dizzy with the scent of his cologne. It wasn't overpowering, just enough to tease her nose with the layered scent of old books and dry pine, with an undernote of something comforting and metallic, like cinnamon warmed in copper. He smelled, she realized as he pulled away, kind of like Cliffside, with its secret corners and tarnished treasures. Like ozone right before the rain that came and washed all the leaves down from the roof. Like her cup of evening tea, steaming into the coolness of the coming night as she watched the spring storms roll in.

"I brought you this," he said, handing her the box as they walked down the hall. He put out a hand to stop her before they reached the kitchen, and she paused, looking at him questioningly.

"Open it here. Not in front of everyone. I, uh, don't know if you'll like them."

For a moment, Emma felt a wave of dread, and she hoped that she wouldn't open the box to find a bouquet of roses.

But she needn't have feared. She set the box on one of the hall tables and carefully unwrapped the simple brown wrapping paper, lifting the lid of the two-piece base and lid inside to reveal a hand-painted sign. The ornately carved wooden sign read, "Welcome to Cliffside," and Emma saw that there were pairs of eyehooks in the top and bottom of the sign. She lifted the sign out to see that another of the same size was below, separated by thin layers of tissue paper. The second sign read, "A Bed and Breakfast." The lettering on each was evocative of hanging shop signs of old, the letters brightly painted and curving in sinuous swoops, highlighted with cream-colored drop shadows.

"I love them," Emma said. "I can't believe you did this."

"Thank Bill," Hudson said. "He knew a guy who does these."

Emma laughed, putting a hand to her heart. It was such a thoughtful gift—in fact, one of the most thoughtful she'd received in years. "He seems to know a guy for everything. Oh, Hudson, these really are something. I'll hang them first thing in the morning."

Then, Emma surprised herself when she turned, put a hand on his shoulder, and stood on tip toes to kiss Hudson Ford on the cheek. She heard his sharp intake of breath, and the equally quick exhale, which sent warmth over her own cheek as she drew away.

"Thank you," she repeated, a little breathless. She started to step back, but Hudson put a hand up, cupping her elbow gently—just enough contact to stop her from moving away. Emma's breath caught. He had stopped her too close to be without intent.

"Emma," he said, and it was one word that somehow managed to say a lot more. He took another breath—this time, slow and deep. "I hope that hanging these means that you're going to stay at Cliffside."

She could hear the other guests, just down the hall, their faint laughter and conversation filtering to where she and Hudson stood. "I—that's the plan."

"Good," he said, shifting even closer. "I was hoping you would say that." She looked up at him, and his eyes dropped to half-shuttered, the focus of the remaining sliver of green *very* obvious to Emma.

Oh my gosh, Hudson Ford is about to kiss me.

Did she want him to kiss her?

As Hudson's head dipped, Emma realized that she *did.*

Time seemed to stretch. Emma might have come up on her toes just the slightest bit.

A million worries flooded her mind as his lips met hers—how unwise it was to get involved with someone now, before her divorce was finalized, how it was way too fast to be this interested in the handsome antiques dealer, and how everyone in this small town would be whispering if they caught any kind of hint that Hudson Ford had kissed the new owner of Cliffside.

And *what* a kiss. The worries flew out of her head as fast as they arrived there, lost under the warm, sure press of Hudson's mouth against hers. The kiss wasn't aggressive. It was gentle, and coaxing, welcoming but restrained, like a banked fire that just warms the hearth on a cold winter night. Emma thought, as he slid his fingers into the hair at the back of her neck, that she had been cold inside for a very long time.

But the quiet moment of passion dissolved in mere heartbeats, disrupted as reality set in. In the other room, someone dropped something that thudded loudly, reminding Emma of the others nearby who could catch them in their embrace. She pulled away, settling back to rest on her heels. There were no words between them—just a silence that Emma wasn't quite sure how to fill.

Hudson cleared his throat as the moment of silence stretched into something slightly awkward. "We should, uh—is everyone…"

"Yes. They're all in the kitchen."

But neither of them moved. Emma picked up the sign box and clutched it close, waiting—her cheeks flaming. Hudson's expression said that he was about to say something. But whatever it was, it never came. He was the very picture of courage being worked up, though, and so Emma stayed and waited patiently. Whatever he had to say couldn't be worse than Troy, or Ed, or ticket cop, or Cousin Nathan.

Finally, Hudson shoved both hands in his coat pockets and looked over her head, down at his feet, past her in the hall—basically, everywhere rather than at her—as he spoke.

"I had a good time at lunch with you that first day," he said to the tapestry to the left of her on the wall. "In fact, I had a good time climbing around the roof with you. I just—I guess I really like hanging out with you in general."

"Me, too," she said.

He forged ahead. "And I know I've teased you about dinner before, but it was also, um, I would also really love"—he sighed, heavily—"I would like to take you out on an official date. If you want."

"Hudson, I can't."

His shoulders tensed. "Yeah, okay. I get it," he said softly to the new hall runner rug. "You have a lot on your plate with the reno, and, really, I *do* understand."

"No, you don't," she said, stepping close and putting her hand back on his shoulder. He looked up from where he was gazing at the floor. She didn't know why, but she trusted Hudson with her story. Sure, it was painful, and it was embarrassing how easily she'd been duped, but Hudson wasn't Troy, and there was no reason she should hide what had happened to her. She could be honest with him—because honesty was what she had been so unjustly denied in her own past.

"Hudson, I'm *married*."

His eyes widened. "*Oh.*" Then, as if for emphasis, he said it again.

Then, he looked from her to the gift box, and she could see the wheels turning in his head. She jostled the box gently. "These are amazing. And no one is coming to beat you up for giving a gift—or a kiss—to his wife. Troy, my soon to be ex-husband, and I are divorcing. As quickly as we can."

"What a moron," Hudson said sharply. Color came into his cheeks now, and she could tell from his expression that he was wrestling with some embarrassment for having kissed her.

Emma froze, surprised by the vehemence in his voice. "What?"

"What kind of pure idiot divorces *you*?" Hudson asked, rocking on his heels. "I mean, you're creative, smart, funny, resourceful, beautiful…"

Emma felt her cheeks flush. "Thank you, but I'm divorcing *him*." She swallowed past a sudden lump in her throat. "He decided he could see other people without informing me."

Hudson's eyes narrowed, and a muscle ticked in his jaw. "I restate—what an irredeemable moron."

Emma licked her dry lips and swallowed around the lump in her throat again. This time, it seemed to stick midway down, and she croaked past it. "I'm telling you this because I like you." She watched his face as she continued. His green eyes stayed on hers, and he waited as patiently for her as she had for him earlier, when he'd been getting up his mettle to ask her out. "And I might *like-like* you in the future, but I can't like-like you right now."

Hudson nodded. "I understand. I'm not here to push you into anything."

"So can we just stay friends? For now?"

His face grew soft and serious. "Emma, we can stay friends even if you never *like-like* me."

"Oh. That's good." Emma relaxed, and she saw that Hudson's shoulders were no longer tense, either. "Should we go show these to everyone?" She held the gift box aloft.

"Ladies first," he said, sweeping a hand toward the empty hall in front of her.

"I thought it was age before beauty?" she replied, gesturing to him to go first.

"Ouch," he said as they started up the hall side by side. "I think I'm going to rethink this offer of friendship. The sparring is already hurting my delicate feelings."

"Too late. No takesies backsies. You're stuck with me unless you leave town."

"Oh, fine. But once your initial trial subscription is up, I'm going to charge you 29.99 a month to hang out with me."

Emma mock winced. "Didn't you hear the whole sad tale? I'm broke. I got robbed by a contractor—who is still at large—my ex wiped out our investment accounts out of spite, and I have put every remaining penny into making this place half livable. The 'breakfast' part of this here bed and breakfast is going to be skim milk and generic corn flakes. Year round."

They emerged from the hallway into the warm light of the kitchen, and Hudson's laughter merged with the chatter of the group already gathered there. "I think today's travelers need to be toughened up a bit, actually, so…"

As they entered the kitchen, laughing together, another wave of noise was set off as everyone called hello to Hudson. Emma smiled again, feeling the warmth of her rediscovered joy fill her and overflow.

On the island, she saw her phone light up. She'd spent so much time during the first part of her time here at Cliffside with her phone turned off that she'd gotten out of the habit of checking it all the time. In fact, until the financial panic that had overcome her after Dusty's scam and Troy's playing bandit with their investment money, she had gotten to a point where she rarely ever carried her phone with her unless she was leaving the house. As Hudson began to make the rounds, Emma picked up the device and swiped to read her email. The alert was something new—it was from her realtor in LA, and the subject line sent a thrill through her—*We have offers over asking price!*

Emma opened the email, holding her breath. There was a small bidding war going on between two buyers. The war had been sparked by—Emma laughed—the art on the walls. Emma's own paintings, which she'd left to be used as staging. Both of the potential buyers were insisting the existing art be retained and included in the final price.

Pip, who was at one end of the dining room table plating cookies warm from the oven, looked over at Emma and smiled. Emma mouthed, "I love you," to her aunt. Pip raised an index finger into the air and traced an invisible heart.

Pip smiled again, more broadly, and handed a cookie to Bill—who leaned over and kissed Pip's cheek, garnering an *Oooo* from Morgan and a *yuck* from Tilly, who pushed in for a cookie of her own. Ethan and Daniel were at the other end of the table, poring together over a robotics manual that Ethan had brought. The two new friends were oblivious to the party going on beside them. Eric and Gerald were discussing city-wide plumbing, and Emma watched her younger niece and nephew toddle around the legs of the gathered adults.

There were still things troubling Emma—the mystery of her parents' past here at Cliffside, which she still had no answers for. The potential forthcoming mess that Dan the Magazine Man would bring down on her fledgling business, potentially killing her chances before she'd even begun. And the lingering worries about money and the divorce that would likely keep her unsettled for months to come.

But Emma was not alone—and she was not incapable, as the past weeks had proven. And despite what Janice had said before Emma had quit VogueThink, there were apt to be more opportunities out there so that Emma could use her skills while completing the rest of the reno and getting Cliffside up and profitable. Ways that she could combine her marketing expertise with her new business so that she could earn as she grew the bottom line of the B and B.

She would start a job search in the morning.

Lola sidled up beside Emma, and pointed to Hudson, who was now chatting with Bill by the sliding glass doors that led to the back gardens. "You brought a date, I see."

"Nah," Emma said, though thinking of Hudson and a real date made the butterflies happy. And remembering the kiss that had just happened in the hall, mere steps from the gathered rest of her company—she had to put a hand to her cheek to try to hide the blush she felt threatening again.

"We're just friends. For now. I feel a little too under construction to be looking for anything new."

Lola nodded. "I guess we're all under construction, aren't we?"

Emma nodded too. "But we've got a good crew." She jostled Lola with her shoulder. Lola gave Emma's arm a pat and went to sit with Daniel and Ethan.

Opening a new, blank email, Emma thumbed out a short but important message. She filled in the email address, hit send, and then powered her phone off, tucking it into her back pocket.

Emma didn't need to see the response come in right now. Maybe not even tomorrow. She had more important things in her life, here at Cliffside.

Here, at *home.*

NOW AVAILABLE!

JUST ONE CHANCE
(A Porch by the Sea—Book 2)

In #1 Bestseller Sophie Love's new sweet romance series, with Memorial Day looming and the grand opening of her new B&B here, Emma Gold finds herself in a furious race against time to finish her renovations. But with a developer intent on stopping her, the renovations going awry, upset guests, and a misunderstanding with her new boyfriend, Emma has to wonder: has she made the right life choice?

"The perfect romance or beach read, with a difference: its enthusiasm and beautiful descriptions offer an unexpected attention to the complexity of not just evolving love, but evolving psyches. It's a delightful recommendation for romance readers looking for a touch more complexity from their romance reads."
--Midwest Book Review (*For Now and Forever*)

JUST ONE CHANCE is Book #2 in a charming new romantic comedy series by bestselling author Sophie Love, whose books have received over 5,000 five-star reviews.

Emma Gold, a high-powered advertising exec from Los Angeles, is used to being in control of her life. She squashed her dreams of being an artist in order to get ahead, and she turned a blind eye to who her husband really was.

But now, with everything falling apart, she realizes there might be more to life.

When Emma is beckoned to visit her aunt, a funny and feisty elderly woman who smokes cigars, drives race cars and owns a massive, crumbling house in a beautiful, quaint seaside town, Emma thinks she is just coming for a weekend. Little does she know her life is about to change.

With her sister living nearby and her aunt needing to move out, Emma wonders if maybe the idea is not so crazy. And when she meets the local antiques dealer, she even has to wonder if there might just be a second chance at love awaiting her.

But Emma is new to renovation, to running a B&B, to dealing with a local zoning board—and to dealing with a distant, hostile relative who wants the house for himself and who will do anything he can to stop her. In a series of laugh-out-loud events, Emma learns that, sometimes, we have to let go of control.

And, sometimes, a new love—and a new life—might just be waiting around the corner.

JUST ONE CHANCE is book #2 in the debut of a funny and dazzling new sweet romance series that will make you laugh, make you cry, will keep you turning pages late into the night—and will make you fall in love with clean romance all over again.

"The romance is there, but not overdosed. Kudos to the author for this amazing start of a series that promises to be very entertaining."
--Books and Movies Reviews (*For Now and Forever*)

Future books in the series are also available!

Sophie Love

#1 bestselling author Sophie Love is author of THE INN AT SUNSET HARBOR romantic comedy series, which includes eight books; of THE ROMANCE CHRONICLES romantic comedy series, which includes 5 books; of the CANINE CASPER cozy mystery series, which includes six books (and counting); of the CURIOUS BOOKSTORE cozy mystery series, which includes five books (and counting); and of the new A PORCH BY THE SEA romantic comedy series, which includes five books (and counting).

Sophie would love to hear from you, so please visit www.sophieloveauthor.com to email her, to join the mailing list, to receive free ebooks, to hear the latest news, and to stay in touch!

BOOKS BY SOPHIE LOVE

A PORCH BY THE SEA
JUST ONE KISS (Book #1)
JUST ONE CHANCE (Book #2)
JUST ONE SUMMER (Book #3)
JUST ONE NIGHT (Book #4)
JUST ONE DAY (Book #5)

A CURIOUS BOOKSTORE COZY MYSTERY
THE WITCHING PLACE: A FATAL FOLIO (Book #1)
THE WITCHING PLACE: MURDER BY MANUSCRIPT (Book #2)
THE WITCHING PLACE: A PERILOUS PAGE (Book #3)
THE WITCHING PLACE: A VANISHED VOLUME (Book #4)
THE WITCHING PLACE: A TAINTED TOME (Book #5)

THE CANINE CASPER COZY MYSTERY SERIES
THE GHOSTLY GROUNDS: MURDER AND BREAKFAST (Book #1)
THE GHOSTLY GROUNDS: DEATH AND BRUNCH (Book #2)
THE GHOSTLY GROUNDS: MALICE AND LUNCH (Book #3)
THE GHOSTLY GROUNDS: VENGEANCE AND DINNER (Book #4)
THE GHOSTLY GROUNDS: SCANDAL AND SUPPER (Book #5)
THE GHOSTLY GROUNDS: DISASTER AND DESSERT (Book #6)

THE INN AT SUNSET HARBOR
FOR NOW AND FOREVER (Book #1)
FOREVER AND FOR ALWAYS (Book #2)
FOREVER, WITH YOU (Book #3)
IF ONLY FOREVER (Book #4)
FOREVER AND A DAY (Book #5)
FOREVER, PLUS ONE (Book #6)
FOR YOU, FOREVER (Book #7)
CHRISTMAS FOREVER (Book #8)

THE ROMANCE CHRONICLES
LOVE LIKE THIS (Book #1)

LOVE LIKE THAT (Book #2)
LOVE LIKE OURS (Book #3)
LOVE LIKE THEIRS (Book #4)
LOVE LIKE YOURS (Book #5)

Printed in Great Britain
by Amazon

31304458R00078